The Dom's Submission

His Mission

Book 2

Ellis O. Day

I love to hear from readers so email me at
authorellisoday@gmail.com

https://www.EllisODay.com

Facebook
https://www.facebook.com/EllisODayRomanceAuthor/

Closed FB Group (sneak peeks, sample chapters, and other bonuses)
https://www.facebook.com/groups/153238782143373

Twitter
https://twitter.com/ellis_o_day

Pinterest
www.pinterest.com\AuthorEllisODay

Ellis O. Day

(AVAILABLE IN PAPERBACK AND EBOOK)

CHAPTER 1: Terry

Terry had found his perfect little sub and wasn't letting Maggie get away that easily. He wasn't tired of fucking her yet. "Why do you have to leave? Your kids don't come home until Sunday."

"I have to work tonight." Maggie looked in the mirror and straightened her hair.

"What time?"

"Five."

"That's hours from now." Which gave him hours to convince her to call off. It was a shitty job anyway.

"I have to pack." She headed into the bedroom.

"Pack?" He followed, watching the way her ass bounced as she walked. God, he wanted to slap that butt and watch it jiggle as he fucked her.

"Yeah, I have to move in a couple of weeks."

"Why?" She'd better not be moving far away. They were nowhere near done with their...It wasn't a relationship, but unlike with his other subs, he hadn't drawn up a contract. It didn't matter what they called it. They were not done with each other.

"Can't afford to stay there since the divorce."

"Where are you moving?"

"Not far." She walked faster into the living room.

That was good, but she was hiding something. As a lawyer, he was quite familiar with evasive answers. He leaned against the dining room table. "Where?"

"Down the street a bit." She looked around the living room. "Have you seen my purse?"

He pointed to the table next to the door.

She walked over and grabbed her phone from her purse.

"What are you doing?"

"Calling an Uber."

"Don't." They'd been over this, again and again. "You can use my car. It's just sitting in the garage."

"I'm not taking your car."

"Why? I don't use it. No one does." He'd never met such a stubborn woman. "I bought it for my daughter as a college graduation present but she wanted a European trip. So, the car sits there." He walked across the room toward her. "You'd be doing me a favor. It's not good for cars to sit. They need to be driven." Like women needed to be fucked. "Plus, you agreed to obey me."

"That's only when...you know." She blushed as she waved her hand. She was adorable.

"When we fuck. Say it." He stepped closer to her, letting her feel the pull of attraction between them.

"No. You know what I meant." She stepped aside and started to punch numbers into her phone.

He snatched it from her.

"Hey, give that back."

He couldn't believe he was reduced to this. He held it in the air out of her reach, as his mind scrambled for a way to make her stay.

"Stop acting like a child and give me my phone."

She was right, but she brought out the worst in him. "If you won't take the car, at least, let me drive you home." He handed her the phone.

She frowned but nodded. "Thank you."

"Give me a moment." He went into his bedroom and came back with his keys and his gym bag. Hopefully, he wouldn't need the change of clothes because of working out. "Ready?"

He opened the door to the garage and stepped aside so she could go first. She eyed the bag but kept her suspicions to herself like a good little sub.

CHAPTER 2: Maggie

Maggie stared out the window as Terry drove her home. This was a mistake. She should've taken an Uber. She was pretty sure he had no intention of going to the gym which meant he'd brought a change of clothes for other reasons. Her body tingled at the thought of another night with him. She dug her nails into her palm, reminding her traitorous body that it was over, no more nights of passion. She got too attached too fast. She wasn't going to make the same mistake again. She had to stop relying on men to help her. She needed to learn to take care of herself.

"So, where are you moving to?"

"Down the road." She wasn't telling anyone except those she had to where she and her children were moving. It was embarrassing. The neighborhood was a dump and she'd cried all night when she'd realized that it was the only place she could afford.

"Is there a reason you won't tell me where?" He glanced at her. "I promise not to show up on your doorstep."

"That's not it." She smiled at him. She was sure she'd fantasize many nights about him arriving at her home and sweeping her off her feet and into his bed.

"Then why are you being so secretive."

"I don't see why it matters." This was going to be hard. "Terry, I appreciate all you've done for me, I do."

"But…" His jaw clenched and his eyes narrowed as he stared at the road ahead of them.

"But I have three kids. I don't have time for a man in my life."

"You had time for one between your legs. Several times."

She inhaled sharply and turned toward the window. He was just like David and every other man, lashing out when he didn't get his way.

He didn't say anything and neither did she but she wanted to. She was always the one who made the peace but she wasn't doing it this time. He'd been cruel and she deserved better than that. He pulled into her driveway and she hopped out.

"Thank you for the ride." Her face heated at his smirk. "For bringing me home. Goodbye."

She slammed the door and hurried toward her house, his footsteps right behind her. She was tempted to run, but that would be undignified. Plus, she'd never make it to the door and inside before he caught up with her.

He stopped next to her on the porch. "When do the movers get here?"

She put her key in the lock and opened the door. "Movers? What movers?"

"You're packing the whole house by yourself?"

She didn't have money for movers. "Yes, and I have a lot to

do." She stepped inside. "Thank you again for helping with my car and bringing me home and—"

"And everything." He moved closer.

She wanted to rest her head against his chest, let him fight her battles and protect her from the world, but that never worked, so instead she took a step back. "Goodbye, Terry."

She started to close the door but he caught it. She stared at him, waiting for him to say something—apologize for being so rude, tell her goodbye, ask to see her again. She'd have to refuse, of course, but she wanted him to ask.

"Do you want some help?"

"What?" She hadn't expected that.

"Packing. I can help." He pushed the door open a little. "Point me in the right direction."

"Ah..." She shouldn't let him. She needed to end this and after his crude comment in the car it'd be the perfect time.

"Come on. This is a lot of work and you could use an extra pair of hands."

That was true. The two older kids tried to help but they made more messes than anything else. "Are you sure?"

"I wouldn't have offered if I didn't want to do it." He stepped inside her house, closing the door behind him. "So, where do we start?"

This was a mistake. She knew it, but she couldn't send him away. Not yet. "I guess little Davy's room. He won't care."

CHAPTER 3: Terry

"What do you mean by that?" Terry had no idea why he was staying to help Maggie, except that he wasn't ready for their day together to end.

"Isabella will care. She's almost eight and she wants to help." She walked down the hallway and he followed.

"Ah, I remember little girls that age." His daughter had been his kryptonite.

She gave him an odd glance over her shoulder.

"My daughter." He slapped her ass.

"Don't start." She walked into the baby's bedroom.

"Then stop thinking I'm a pervert." He had to repair the damage his big mouth and temper had caused.

"I wasn't." She handed him a box from the corner. "Toys."

"Yes, ma'am." He started filling the box. "You know, I'm the one who's supposed to be in charge."

"Only in the bedroom." She averted her eyes but her face turned a rosy hue.

"We're in a bedroom."

"Oh, we are." Her eyes widened. "But not to...you know."

"We could." He definitely could.

"Bed's too small."

"We don't need a bed and you know it." He moved to a toy box. "I'm sure you remember, we fucked on the bathroom counter." He opened the lid. "We can load this as is, right?" It was her house and her stuff, so he needed to ask.

"No. Too heavy."

He bent and lifted it. "Not for me." He straightened, liking the appreciation on her face. "Where to?"

"Garage. I'll get the door."

"Don't worry about it." He wanted her impressed with his strength. It'd make her wet. It might even help her forget his earlier comment.

"You sure?"

"Yep." He hefted it a little higher. Damn, the thing was kind of heavy but there was no way he was letting her know that. "Where?"

"Door to the garage is through the kitchen."

"Got it." He strode out of the room and into the kitchen. It wasn't easy propping the toy box against the wall and opening the door, but he managed. He was a man after all. He placed it near a stack of boxes.

He went back to the bedroom and began unloading a dresser, staring at the little clothes in his hands. It'd been a long time since he'd touched clothes this size.

Babies were so helpless and yet so determined–forcing him and his wife to change their lives and he'd loved every minute. One of the shirts had a faded stain—puke. He stuffed it in the box with the other clothes. Okay, he hadn't loved *every* minute, not the late nights nor when they'd been sick or the toys scattered all around the house. Both him and his wife had been too tired to do anything but crash in the bed—no sex, no talking, just exhausted sleep. He didn't need to do this again. He didn't want to do this again. He'd raised his kids. He was done.

He quickly filled the box and took it to the garage, coming back and taking the one she'd packed. He should go. He'd fucked her and now he could forget her. He'd tell her he had to leave. That work had called. He walked into the bedroom.

She straightened, pushing her hair from her face. "Okay, I think we've done as much as we can. I still need some things out until moving day. We should do Peter's room next." She moved past him into the bedroom across the hall.

He followed. This was a little boy's room filled with cars and balls and action figures. His son had loved all those things when he was little. Right before his divorce. Right before he'd become a visitor in his kids' lives.

She looked around and grabbed a box. "This is going to take a while." She smiled at him. "Thanks for helping."

"You're welcome." Only a real asshole would leave her to do this alone. He'd help until she had to go to work and then this was over.

She bent and picked up some toys. His gaze rested on her ass. Who was he kidding? He wasn't done with her yet. They were adults, engaging in a casual arrangement. He didn't need to ever be around her kids. They could meet during the day or at night, whenever she had an hour or so and…"How often does your ex take the kids?"

"He's supposed to take them every other weekend but sometimes he skips." She frowned. "Too busy."

"That's bullshit."

She stared at him.

He shrugged. "I always made time for my kids, no matter how busy I was."

"You were a good father."

He had been a good father. He'd read to them. Watched cartoons with them. He'd hated the shows but loved their giggles and the way they'd climb onto his lap—their little bodies snuggled against him, one on each side. And then they were gone, except every other weekend.

He didn't want to count the Saturdays he'd spent watching those stupid kid shows by himself, missing his children. He needed to get away from this room, those memories. "I need a drink."

"I have water, milk and juice."

He needed a shot or two but even a beer would do. "No beer? Any alcohol?"

"No. Sorry."

"Water then. You want one?"

"Yeah, thanks."

He went into the kitchen and grabbed two bottles from the refrigerator. He took a deep breath, staring at nothing but seeing his past. All those nights alone. He'd stayed at the office late every day. He'd had to start a new business and that took a lot of time but he also hadn't wanted to go home.

"Terry, did you find the water?" Maggie yelled from the other room.

He could do this. He could pack those toys and those little clothes. He could keep those memories—all the lonely days, weekends, and holidays—at bay. Unless..."Do you want me to start in the kitchen," he hollered. "We could tackle two rooms at once."

She came to the door. "If you want. Are you okay?"

"Yeah. Of course." He handed her a bottle of water.

"Okay." She was looking at him, an odd expression on her face.

"We can finish the bedroom if you prefer. I just thought I could get the heavier kitchen items."

"Yeah, silverware and dishes are very heavy."

"They are if you pack a box full of them." He didn't need her smart mouth right now.

"You can work in the kitchen or anywhere you like. I just appreciate the help." She turned, walking back toward the bedroom but he was pretty sure he'd seen hurt in her big, hazel eyes.

"No. You're right. We should do one room at a time." Even if it killed him. He'd remember her face as he'd slid his dick inside of her. She wasn't a mother then. She was just the woman he was fucking.

CHAPTER 4: Maggie

Maggie picked up their plates as Terry tossed the last bite of his peanut butter and jelly sandwich into his mouth. It'd been all she'd had at the house for a late lunch. Maybe, she should've let him order takeout like he'd offered. "Sorry that I didn't have anything else."

"Are you kidding? I forgot how good PB&J was. I used to eat it with my kids all the time." His eyes grew a little sad and distant.

"I'm glad you enjoyed it." She doubted he had, but he was being an excellent sport. Like it or not, he was a nice guy.

"Where next?" he asked.

"I guess my room."

"Excellent." He grinned, his dark eyes roaming over her hungrily.

"We're packing. That's it." She headed down the hallway, feeling better already.

"I've got something you can pack," he whispered by her ear.

She shivered but elbowed him in the gut. "We don't have time."

"We can make time."

She turned around. This had to stop. "Terry, if that's why you're helping—"

"It's not." He shrugged. "Not entirely anyway. I mean, I wouldn't turn you down."

"That's honest." She laughed.

He took her chin in his grasp. "Always. I told you that. I may be blunt and thoughtless, sometimes even cruel, but I'm always honest." His eyes searched hers. "And I'm sorry I was cruel."

It wasn't the best apology she'd ever gotten but she was pretty sure it was the best she'd get from this arrogant, controlling man.

"Okay, but I have a lot to do and very little time."

"When are you moving?" He grabbed an empty box from the corner.

"We have to be out of here in a week."

"And you're going to pack the entire house?" He didn't even try to hide his disbelief.

"I've done a lot already." She pointed to the closet. "Start there. Put everything in the box."

"Why don't you hire someone to help you?" He dropped the box on the floor.

"You want the truth?" She wasn't sure why she was willing to tell him. It was embarrassing.

"Always." He stopped putting clothes in the box and stared at her.

"I can't afford it." She bent, starting with the bottom dresser drawer so she didn't have to see the look of pity on his face.

"I can pay for it."

"No. Thank you, but that's not why I told you." She couldn't take his money.

"I know that. I want to help. Let me."

She glanced up and he was watching her. "No." She liked him as a friend...with benefits and she wouldn't jeopardize that. She had to end this but she didn't want either of them to have bad memories of their time together. "I can't. I won't borrow—"

"It'll be a gift."

"For what?"

He blinked, stunned.

"Gifts are supposed to be for something—a birthday, Christmas, something."

"Can't a man give a woman a gift for no other reason than he wants to. Because he was thinking of her."

"Well, yes. That might work for a flowers or candy or even jewelry but not movers."

"How about because I care for you and..."

"Stop. Please. You barely know me."

"I know you intimately." His voice deepened, sending shivers racing through her body.

"That's not the same as caring about someone."

"Are you saying that you don't care about me?" He moved toward her. "That you were only using me for my cock."

"No." She should step away. Get back to work but she didn't do either. She stood, waiting for him.

"Of course, my mouth and hands, played"—his eyes dropped to her breasts—"a big part in what we did."

"That's not what I meant." She stepped aside, putting the

box between them. "I do like you."

His eyes darkened even more.

"As a friend." Now, his lips were drawn and tight, and she wanted nothing more than to press against them—make them and her happy—but she couldn't. "And that's why I can't let you do this. It wouldn't be right. I don't take money from friends."

"How about fuck-buddies? Do you take money from them?"

"There's no reason to be crass."

"Right. No reason at all." He went back to the other side of the room and resumed stuffing items from the closet into the box.

He was obviously pissed but she wasn't backing down on this. Still, she didn't like tension. She'd never liked fighting. "Look, I'm sorry that I won't take your money."

"You think that's why I'm mad." He threw a handful of her clothes into the almost full box.

"Well, yeah. I assumed you didn't like not getting your way." He certainly didn't in the bedroom.

"I don't but that's not...Forget it. You're right." He closed the box and picked it up, carrying it out of the room.

CHAPTER 5: Terry

Terry left the bedroom as quickly as he could. Getting away from Maggie was the only way for him to keep his cool. *Friends.* She thought of him as a friend. That was like a slap in the nuts. He'd fucked her six ways till Sunday. His lips curled in a grin. He was going to fuck her tonight and throughout Sunday. But friends? He dropped the box by the stack of others. He hadn't paid attention before but there were a lot of boxes in this garage and that meant she'd packed all of them by herself. This was crazy. She shouldn't be doing this alone and how was she going to move everything to her new house? She didn't even have a car. He pulled his phone from his pocket. Time to call in some debts.

By the time he made it back to the bedroom he was in a much better mood. His friends would be here tomorrow to help finish packing and when that was done, they'd move it to her new house. She couldn't refuse because it wasn't going to cost him a penny, except for the moving van, but too bad. She needed help and he liked helping her.

The sound of Led Zeppelin drifted down the hallway. His little rabbit kept getting better and better. Classic rock was his favorite type of music. He walked into the bedroom. She was still working at her dresser. He grabbed another box and went back to the closet.

"I do appreciate you helping me with this." She glanced at him.

"That's what friends do." He almost choked on the word— so much for feeling better about this situation.

"Is that why you're upset?"

"Let's not talk about it." He tossed the rest of her clothes in the box. "There's still room in here. Where to next?"

"I didn't mean to hurt your feelings when—"

"You didn't hurt my feelings." Please, he was a grown man not a child.

"Well, I said something that bothered you and I didn't mean to."

"I'm fine." And done talking about this crap. He moved over by the chest of drawers to finish filling his box.

"I'll get that," she snapped and then smiled at him. "Why don't you start in the kitchen like you'd suggested earlier?"

"Sure. As soon as I fill this box." Great. Now, she wanted him working in the other room. He grabbed the handle and she raced across the room, shoving the drawer shut and blocking it with her body.

"Oh, now, I have to see what's in here." He tried to push her out of his way, but she clung to the dresser and she was stronger than she looked.

"Please, Terry. Don't." She looked at him over her shoulder, her eyes pleading.

"What are you hiding? Do you have your ex's body in here or something?" His body pressed deliciously against hers and his dick wanted to come out and play.

"Stop it. Please." She tried to push him away with her back and stilled. She had to feel his cock against her ass.

He shifted his hips to make sure she felt every painful inch of him. He leaned down so his lips brushed against her ear, "Let me see inside the dresser or take off your pants."

"We can't. I have a lot of work—"

"I think it's Sir, right now, don't you?" He kissed her neck, letting his tongue tickle her skin before sucking on it. She was so damn sweet. Her breathing was shallow and her body tense with anticipation. She wanted him as much as he wanted her.

"We can't," she repeated but her words were husky with desire.

"Then step aside and let me see inside your dresser." He unbuttoned his pants. praying that she was too embarrassed to show him whatever was in there because right now he needed to sink his cock inside her. He was going to prove to her that he was a lot of things but her friend wasn't one of them.

"Fine." Her body trembled as she stepped aside.

He stared after her as she walked away. It was like being denied water from a lake that stood right in front of him. She was back at her dresser, filling her box with clothes like he hadn't just about had his dick shoved so deep inside her all she could do was moan.

"Look. You wanted to see what was in there. Look and get it over with."

"I did but given the choice, I'd rather have fucked you." He buttoned his pants.

Her eyes drifted over his body and rested for one blissful second on the bulge straining at his jeans. "I don't have time."

"I could make it quick." He put his hand on the dresser drawer as an incentive. She really hadn't wanted him to see whatever was in there, which made him crazy curious but he could persuade her to show him after he fucked her. "We'd hardly lose any time at all."

"A quickie? Is that supposed to entice me?"

"I'd make sure you enjoyed it. It'd be fast and hard, rough even but filled with pleasure for both of us."

Her lips parted and her breath came a little faster. She just needed a nudge.

"I'd slide my hand between your legs." His eyes held hers. "Maybe, not even unbutton your pants. That way my hand would be tight against you. Only able to move a little. You'd feel every inch of my hand and fingers pressing against you, stroking you."

"Stop." She stepped back, shaking her head slightly. "I'm going to get some water. I'll bring you back some." She fled from the room.

"Run, my little rabbit," he mumbled to himself. "I'll catch you later." Delaying would make it better. "I'll take a look at what's in your dresser while I wait for you to hop back in here."

He opened the drawer. There was nothing in here but sheets, cloth napkins and table cloths. She'd tricked him. He started to shut the drawer, but the partially empty box loomed at his feet. He never left a job half-finished. He pulled out a pile of linen and tossed them in the box. He grabbed another bunch and stilled. Something hard was wrapped inside them. He dug through the material and grinned. He recognized that shape. He unraveled the cloth, pulling out his prize. His little rabbit had her own Rabbit Vibrator. His dick, which had barely calmed down, clamored for attention and he knew the bunny for the job.

CHAPTER 6: Maggie

Maggie stood in her kitchen, holding a bottle of cold water against her forehead. Damn, Terry. She didn't have time for this. She knew she shouldn't have let him in the house. Now, all she wanted to do was touch him and have him touch her—to feel like a woman again. And oh, those orgasms...She'd give up chocolate for one of those.

"You've been a naughty girl." His rich, dark voice sent desire racing down her spine and coiling between her legs.

"We can't." She put on her sternest face and turned toward him. His delicious smile and the heat in his dark eyes made her knees buckle but the vibrator—her vibrator, her secret shame—in his hands made her want to run from the room. This was so embarrassing. She'd been married. If her husband had wanted her, she wouldn't have needed a vibrator.

"We can." He moved forward. "We will."

"Not, now. I have to get this house packed and—"

"And we will. Later."

He was so close she could smell him, male and soap–

delicious.

"Take off your clothes and get on the table."

She shook her head but her hands started moving to her shirt when her phone rang.

"Leave it." He grabbed her wrist, stopping her from pulling it from her pants pocket.

"It could be my kids."

He let go of her hand, frowning.

She answered without checking to see who it was. "Hello. Oh. Yeah. I guess. Okay." She hung up, staring at the phone. That'd been a mistake.

"Was it your kids? Is everything okay?"

"Yes. I mean, no it wasn't my kids but yes, everything is fine."

"Good." He took the phone and put it on the counter. "Now, get naked and on the table."

She bit her lip. He wasn't going to be happy about this. She wasn't happy about this. "I can't. That was work. I have to go in early."

"What?" The disbelief in his tone almost made her laugh.

"It was work," she repeated. "They asked me to come in early."

"Tell them no."

"I already said yes."

"Call them back and cancel."

"I can't."

"Sure, you can." He grabbed her phone, handing it to her. "Tell them you have plans"—his eyes roamed over her body— "because you do."

"I can't. I'm sorry." She truly was. Even though she didn't

have time for it, she'd wanted to have sex.

"Maggie, you can tell them no." He grinned. "You just can't tell me no." His smile slipped away. "Which is what you're doing."

"I'm sorry." She kind of wasn't. Telling him no was fun.

"Do you want to be punished?" The heat from his gaze almost made her melt.

"No." She glanced up at him. So far, she'd liked everything he'd done to her. "Okay. Maybe a little."

"That can be arranged." His smile was hot enough to melt bone.

"But I can't cancel. I've called out too much already and I need the money."

"I'll pay you." He pulled out his wallet. "What do you make? Ten? Fifteen bucks an hour?" He counted out two hundred dollars and tossed it on the counter. "Now, call them back and then get out of those clothes and onto the table."

She stared at the money. This is what he thought of her. She shouldn't be surprised. He'd met her at a sex club and she hadn't even known him a week before she'd jumped into his bed. "Get out."

"What?"

"You heard me. Get out." She couldn't be around him. Not now. Not after this. She pushed past him. She would not cry. Not yet. Not until he left.

"Maggie." He followed her. "I didn't mean it like that."

"Go away." She walked into her bedroom and slammed the door. It may have even hit his nose by his grunt and then swearing, but she wouldn't feel bad. He deserved that and more.

"Damnit." He flung open the door.

"Go home. I need to shower and go to work."

"Maggie, listen to me." He grabbed her arm.

"Don't you dare touch me." She jerked free. "I am not your whore. You can't pay me to...to..." She couldn't say the words. It was too horrible, too embarrassing.

"I know that." He stepped closer. "I didn't mean it like that. I swear." He ran his hands down her shoulders to her elbows and pulled her toward him. "You know me better than that."

"I don't know you at all." She moved away from him, blinking back the tears. "Th-thank you for your help today but you...you need to leave." She was making a mess of this.

His mouth tightened as if fighting to keep the words in but then he took a deep breath. "I'll give you a ride to work."

"No, thank you. I'll call Uber." Her voice was still crackly with unshed tears but her words were clipped. "Goodbye, Terry."

"Fuck that. You can't dismiss me like a damn child." He stepped closer to her. "I apologized. I didn't offer you the money because I thought I could buy you." He grinned but it wasn't friendly. "Trust me, if I thought money would open your legs, I would've handed you my wallet the first night I met you and I'd be tired of you by now."

It was worse than a slap. She spun around, hurrying to the bathroom and locking the door behind her. She sat on the toilet, his words echoing through her head.

"Son-of a bitch." His footsteps moved to the door. "I didn't mean that. Fuck me." Something hit the door. She was pretty sure it was his head. "Maggie..."

She turned on the shower so she wouldn't hear him and he

wouldn't hear her cry.

CHAPTER 7: Terry

Terry sat on Maggie's bed, waiting. He'd fucked up big time. The money had been a huge mistake but he hadn't been thinking about anything but her and that vibrator. Did she think of him when she used it? How often did she need to get off? He'd be happy to help whenever she felt the urge.

All he'd wanted was her naked but his damn temper had gotten the better of him. He flopped back on the bed. He hadn't snapped like that in years. He would've sworn he'd outgrown it, but it'd hurt when she'd called him a friend and then she'd had the audacity to claim she didn't know him. What the hell did she need to know? He'd saved her at the Club. He'd rescued her when her car broke down. He'd fixed every problem she'd had and yet she didn't know him. That was bullshit.

The shower turned off. He sat up, taking a deep breath and getting a firm hold on his temper. This wasn't over.

She stepped out of the bathroom and froze when her eyes landed on him. Whereas, he didn't know where to look first. The damp towel clung to her curves, hinting at all that soft, rounded flesh that was begging for his touch. God, she looked good and smelled even better. She must use vanilla soap or shampoo and he wanted to gobble her up. His eyes caressed the smooth, bare skin of her legs. That was exactly where he wanted to start tasting her.

"Why are you still here?" She moved to her dresser. The one she'd been cleaning earlier and pulled out some clothes.

"I said, I'd take you to work."

"And I said I'd call an Uber."

"I thought you were broke." Damnit, by the glare she shot him that was the exact wrong thing to say.

"My finances are none of your business." She moved toward the bathroom.

"Wait, please." He stood.

"Why?" She turned toward him.

"I don't want this to end."

"It's already over." She started to walk into the bathroom but he was there before she took two steps.

"I'm sorry about what I said."

"No, you're sorry that I got mad."

"No. Really." He took her hand. "I didn't mean the money like that. I truly didn't. I just didn't want you to leave."

"Well, I have to."

"I know." He tangled his fingers with hers, relishing the softness of her skin. "Forgive me?"

"Terry…"

"Come on. I goofed." He moved a little closer and when she didn't back away, he took it as a good sign. "I'm a stupid male."

"You are that." She glanced down but he swore there was

humor in her tone.

"Help me be better." This would appeal to her giving nature.

"Maybe, I should punish you." Her eyes met his.

"Oh, that reminds me."

"About what?" Her cocky look took on a hint of panic.

"You still need your punishment for coming this morning before I gave you permission."

"You were serious about that?"

"Absolutely." He bent and kissed her. It was too quick but he didn't have much time. "Wait here." He hurried to the door and stopped "And don't put on your pants."

"We don't have time—"

"Trust me." He winked and left.

He hurried to his car and grabbed the package he'd tossed into his gym bag before they'd left his house. He went back into her bedroom.

She was drying her hair, wearing only her shirt and the towel wrapped around her waist. Her panties and pants were lying on the bed. God, she was a natural submissive. He needed to train her to trust him and follow his command all the time, not just sexually. He walked up behind her and her eyes met his in the mirror. He handed her the box. "Your punishment." He bent and kissed her neck, her pulse increasing under his lips. "Open it."

She turned off the blow dryer, placing it on the dresser and took the box. "Ben Wa balls? What are those?"

"Open it and I'll show you." He kissed a trail down her neck, shifting her shirt out of his way.

"Terry, we can't. I don't have time." But she tipped her

head, giving him better access.

"I know, but I wish we could."

"I don't think that we should—"

"Open the package." There was no way she was turning him down tonight, not after wearing these for hours.

She opened the box and took out the toy, eyeing the two balls connected by a cord. "What is this?"

"Let me show you." He took them from her and opened his mouth, letting them slide inside and get nice and slick. He tugged the towel and it fell to the floor.

"We can't…"

Her protest died on her lips as his fingers found her pussy. "You need to be nice and wet." He used two fingers to stroke her on both sides but didn't slip inside. "You're already wet for me, but I think you could be wetter. What do you think?"

"Yes." She rested her head against his shoulder.

"Is that how you're supposed to address me?" He wished he had time to punish her for forgetting, but this would have to do.

"Sorry, Sir."

"That's a good rabbit." She turned her face and he captured her mouth as his finger slipped inside her. She was so hot and ready for him. He should drop his pants and fuck her quick, but then she wouldn't be punished. He lowered his other hand with the toy and rolled the balls over her clit.

"Oh…" She clutched at his wrist, keeping him between her legs.

"Remember, you're supposed to say Yellow when you can't take any more."

"Yes." She tried moving his hand so the balls pressed

against her, but he was stronger than she was.

"This is your punishment." He slid the balls between her aching sex and pushed them inside of her.

"Oh…" She stiffened.

He made sure both were in there nice and far with the string for removal hanging outside her body before stepping away.

"What?" She glanced down and then at him. "You put them inside me?"

"Yes." He sat on the bed, his cock hard and throbbing. "Now, put on your pants."

"We aren't…you know." She was flushing again and he loved it.

"No. Not now." He licked his fingers.

"Oh…but…" She clamped her mouth shut.

"You're wet and aching and need my dick. Don't you?"

Her lips tightened.

"Say it. Tell me the truth, little rabbit or I'll make you suffer longer tonight." He smirked. "And I don't think you're ready for anything more than the Ben Wa balls. Not yet." He'd love to use the vibrator on her while she had the toy inside. He would if she'd stay home. Instead, he'd have to wait. His gaze rested at the juncture between her thighs. The one place in the world he most wanted to be. Would be. Later.

"You expect me to keep them inside me," she whispered the last two words.

"All night." He forced his eyes up to hers. "They only come out when I take them out."

"But what if I have to go to the bathroom?"

"Then, you go, but pee slowly so you don't push them out."

"I can't wear these and work."

"You can and you will." He leaned back on the bed, his dick telling him to fuck her fast but his mind was going to win this battle. His dick would win the war. "You will learn to obey me."

"Terry." Her lips thinned. "Fine."

"I'll know if you remove them."

"How would you know?" Her eyes narrowed. The little cheat had been planning on doing exactly that.

"I'll know. Trust me." He stared at her pussy. "Now, you'd better get dressed before you don't make it to work."

"Oh, right." She seemed to just realize that she wasn't wearing pants. She took a step toward the bed and stopped, her eyes almost popping from her head.

He couldn't stop the grin. "Like that do you?" The quaint little balls moved inside her, hitting all the right spots.

"Yes...No. I can't wear these at work," she almost hissed.

"You can." He stood, no longer able to stay away from her. "And I want you to think about me every time you feel them move."

She stepped around him and grabbed her underwear, pulling them on and moaning. "They move whenever I move," she snapped.

"Good. That means you'll be thinking about me a lot."

She pulled on her pants. "Oh, I'll be thinking about what an ass you are."

He grinned and leaned down so his lips were a breath away from hers. "And I'll be thinking about taking you from behind and then in the ass."

Her breath hitched. "We are not doing that."

"We will later. After I've prepared you and you'll like it." He

31

kissed her, letting his lips linger for one long moment before giving her a healthy swat on the butt.

Her squeak became a small moan as the motion made the balls move inside her.

"Come, little rabbit. Let me take you to work."

CHAPTER 8: Terry

Terry sat in Ethan's office playing cards but he was losing because his mind was on Maggie. She'd feel those balls shifting inside her with every step. He glanced at his watch. She'd been at work a few hours. She'd be soaked and horny with no outlet, until tonight. He'd take his time removing the toy—his smirk died on his lips—unless she'd taken it out. She'd better not have. He tossed his cards down. "I'm hungry." For pussy, but he wasn't going to say that. Ethan would suggest going downstairs into the Club and he was in no mood to explain that he wanted Maggie not just a willing playmate. It'd bring up too many questions and too much bullshit, especially with Nick getting engaged and Patrick now living with Annie.

"Order something." Ethan shuffled.

"No. I want to go to Outback."

Ethan's blue eyes met his over the table. "Outback?"

He should've left. Not only did Ethan have a Michelin star chef working at the Club but the bastard remembered everything.

"The steaks are better here or is it something besides food that you're hungry for?" Ethan grinned.

"I'm going." He stood. He was too old for this bullshit. If he wanted to fuck a specific woman he wasn't going to sit around and listen to Ethan give him shit about it. "If you're coming, keep your mouth shut."

"That'd make it hard to eat." Ethan stood, grabbing his phone. "Hey, Julie. I'm going out for a bit. Watch the Club."

"I mean it. I don't want to hear a damn thing." He headed toward the door.

"Oh, poor Terry can't take being teased. You sure gave it good to Nick though."

"That was completely different. That dumbass was being celibate. Celibate! For a woman he'd just met." He walked down the hallway and into the elevator. "I'm being the exact opposite of celibate with Maggie."

"So, you've trapped and tapped your little pet."

He just smiled. He wasn't a fuck and tell kind of guy.

When they arrived at the restaurant Maggie was seating a group of four. A long line of customers waited for tables.

"Let's eat in the bar," he said.

"You sure." Ethan glanced at Maggie. "She can't ignore you if she has to seat you."

"Please. She's not going to ignore me." He almost hoped she'd try. He'd enjoy punishing her later.

The tables were filled so they took seats at the bar. He shifted so he had a good view of the hostess station. The bartender came by, took their drink orders and dropped off menus. He didn't even pretend to look at it. His eyes were on Maggie as she walked back to her station. She looked around as if sensing his gaze. Her large, hazel eyes widened when she spotted him and her step faltered. Her lips parted slightly and he grinned. Tonight, was going to be fun. The balls were working their magic, rubbing inside her, making her clench those muscles to hold the toy in place. His gaze roamed down her lush body. She was such a good little sub and he couldn't wait to reward her.

Pink tinged her cheeks as she turned away. She led a couple to a table. She was rumpled and sexy as hell. Strands of her misbehaving hair had already escaped the bun and were tucked behind her ear. She wore black slacks that hugged her curves and a white blouse. These clothes fit her and she looked fabulous. His hands itched to run up her thighs to that round ass. It'd jiggle a bit when he slapped it and better yet, it be a soft cradle when he fucked her from behind.

"You ready to order?" asked the bartender.

"New York Strip. Medium rare with baked potato and a salad. Italian dressing on the side." He slid the menu across the bar and picked up his drink.

Ethan ordered and then turned, leaning against the bar. "So, what are your plans? Stay here all night like a stalker?"

"No, but I do need to be back later to give her a ride home."

"Oh, I bet you do." Ethan chuckled.

Maggie returned to her station, glancing at him before saying something to a group of customers and making her way to the bar.

"Terry, Ethan, what are you doing here?" She didn't look

happy to see him. That was going to change.

"I'm hungry. You sell food," he said.

"Oh, right. Of course." She glanced at her station.

He leaned close to whisper. "And I wanted to see if you were enjoying your punishment." He let his lips brush against her ear and pleasure shot straight to his dick when she shivered. *Oh, she wanted him and she was so going to get him.*

"About that." She snapped, turning her face toward his and stepping back when their lips almost touched.

"Yes." He waited, knowing what was coming.

"I can't keep this...I can't wear it any longer." She shifted on her feet, her eyes drifting half-closed from the pleasure of the balls moving inside her. "I can't concentrate."

"You should've obeyed this morning."

"Terry." She glanced around and lowered her voice so much he could barely hear her. "I'm taking it out."

"You'd better not." He touched her chin, so she met his gaze. "I'm not kidding about this." He leaned by her ear again. "It's your punishment and you need to see it through."

"You won't even know." A customer came in and she turned to walk back to her station.

He grabbed her arm. "I'll know." His hand slid down to her wrist, his thumb caressing the entire trip. "I can see it in your face."

"I'll remove it when you leave." She pulled free and strode back to her station.

"Change of plans." He glanced at Ethan. "We're drinking here tonight."

CHAPTER 9: Maggie

Maggie was going to kill Terry. That toy inside her was bad enough but having his dark gaze on her every time she moved was making her insides purr. As soon as he left, that thing was coming out.

She seated the next group of people, the little balls rolling and shifting with each movement and making her almost moan. Who in their right mind designed something like this and why had she let Terry put it inside her? Because she'd wanted him too badly to think and she wanted him even more now. She glanced into the bar on the way back to her station and his eyes captured hers. He grinned, slow and sexy. Her legs trembled and her pussy clenched the Ben Wa balls, wishing they were bigger and longer, wishing they were his dick. His eyes darkened as if he could read her thoughts and her face heated so badly, she wanted to fan herself—or stick her head in the ice bin behind the bar.

She looked away from his hungry, knowing gaze and hurried to her station. Things had slowed down a little. She could take a quick break. She stopped her manager. "Can you cover the door for a minute? I need to use the restroom."

"Sure," said Mary Lou.

She hurried to the back. This thing was coming out before she crumbled to a hot mess in the middle of the dining room.

CHAPTER 10: Terry

"I'll be right back." Terry finished his drink. "Get me another."

"I've got to get back to the Club." Ethan waved the bartender over. "Get my friend another and I need to settle up."

"I've got it." Terry glanced toward the back where Maggie had disappeared. He had to stop his little rabbit from misbehaving.

"Thanks. Have fun." Ethan grinned as he stood.

"Oh, I plan on it." Terry walked over to the woman at Maggie's station. "Excuse me, where are the restrooms?"

"Down there to the right." Her eyes trailed over him as she pointed in the direction Maggie had gone.

"Do the employees use those facilities too?"

"Yes, but you're not—"

"Thanks." He strode through the restaurant. People often answered questions on instinct, not thinking just talking. He'd won many a case on that alone. He stepped into the men's room and counted to five. He walked back into the hallway, glancing into the dining room. Perfect. The woman who was watching Maggie's station was seating a group of six. He moved to the ladies' room and pushed the door open a crack. "Maggie, you in there?"

"Terry?" she squeaked.

"Are you alone?"

"Go away."

He opened the door and peeked inside. Only one stall was occupied and there was no one else in the room. He closed the door behind him. Unfortunately, there wasn't a lock. "You'd better not be taking out the Ben Wa balls."

"You can't be in here."

"But I am." He tapped on the stall. "Let me in and prove that you're not being a naughty girl."

"You're going to get me fired."

He hoped that happened. Then, they could be at his house fucking, but he knew better than to say that. "Not if you do as I say." He tapped on the door again. "Hurry up. Some lady is bound to need to pee soon."

CHAPTER 11: Maggie

Maggie flushed the toilet and stepped out of the stall. Part of her wanted to kill him for his arrogance, but a bigger part of her wanted to jump him. She was hornier than she'd ever been in her life and it didn't help that he was so damn handsome.

His tall, fit body was on display in those expensive clothes that accented his muscular chest and slim hips and his stern features lit up when he smiled. She wanted to tear off her clothes and let him take her right here–a quickie in the bathroom. What was happening to her? She'd never, ever thought things like this but with those balls tucked inside her, wiggling with every movement, all she wanted was sex.

"Wash your hands."

"I was going to." But she'd gotten sidetracked with her fantasies. She walked to the sink, squirted soap in her hand and turned on the water. He stepped behind her, so close she could feel the heat from his body.

"You still have them in." His eyes met hers in the mirror.

It wasn't a question but she nodded anyway, mesmerized

by his dark, hot look.

"But you came in here to take them out. Didn't you?"

She finished washing her hands and started to straighten, but his arm wrapped around her, lifting her as he stepped backward into the stall.

"Close the door." His voice was thick and rough, drawing her into sensual quicksand.

She shut the stall door and locked it.

"Brace yourself on the door." His hand pressed against the small of her back and she obeyed.

He grabbed her hips and yanked her backward, her ass now resting against his groin. She whimpered at the feel of his hard cock. She couldn't stop from wiggling against him. She didn't mean to but her body was so on edge, so needy.

"I could fuck you hard and fast, right here." His hand trailed up her spine and around to her front, skimming over her breasts before skating, too quickly, over her pussy.

"Please." She no longer cared if they got caught. All she cared about was releasing the pressure that'd been building in her all night.

He leaned down so his lips brushed her ear and his dick rubbed against her ass. "You'd like that wouldn't you? My hard cock, slamming into you over and over until you came, right here in the bathroom." His hand cupped between her legs.

"Yes." She grabbed his wrist, pushing it against her. It wouldn't take much and she'd come.

"You never answered my question." He rubbed softly not giving any relief, only teasing touches making her hornier.

"Yes. I'd like you to take me hard and fast, right here. Please. Terry. Sir. Master." She couldn't think straight. All her focus was on how much she needed his touch.

"That's better, but that's not the question."

She looked at him over her shoulder. "What question?"

"You came in here to remove your punishment, didn't you?"

His hand was driving her mad, fleeting touches and she needed so much more. She wiggled her ass again and his face tensed.

"You'll pay for that later." He swatted her butt and she jumped but the slight pain made her want him more.

The main bathroom door opened and two women came inside, chatting.

"Shhh." He whispered as he braced his hands on the wall and stood on the toilet.

Her heart pounded in her ears. Oh, god, if they got caught, she'd get fired. This was crazy. She'd been going to have sex in the restroom. That was public indecency.

The women each went into a stall and Terry wrapped his hand around her throat, pulling her toward him. He squatted on the toilet and she stood between his knees, as his hungry mouth kissed her neck and his naughty hand slid over her abdomen and between her legs, making her clench down on the balls inside of her.

One woman flushed and then the other. They both washed their hands, chatting as they left. Maggie hadn't been able to understand a word, her mind exploding with passion.

He stepped off the toilet, keeping her near. "Answer my question. Did you come in here to remove your punishment?" He nipped her ear and unbuttoned her pants. He slid his hand inside, slipping his fingers between her slick folds.

"Oh…" She was going to come. She rocked against him. She needed this. It could be quick.

"Answer me and I'll know if you're lying, so don't."

She didn't want to tell him the truth. He'd be mad but she was pretty sure he already knew the answer. "Yes. I had to. I'm so…I can't take it anymore."

"You're so what?" He kissed her ear. "Say it."

"Horny. I'm so damn horny." It'd only take a moment. She clutched his wrist, mentally begging him to slip one finger inside of her.

"That's good." He straightened, pulling his hand from her pants. He swatted her ass, but this time it was more playful. "Go back to work. Finish your shift and then you can have my cock." He opened the stall and strode to the main door. "And don't take them out. I'll do that later."

Her legs trembled and he laughed as he left. Damn him. These were coming out and she was not going home with him tonight, or ever again. It was over. She was done with overbearing, dominant assholes.

CHAPTER 12: Terry

Terry walked back to the bar and grabbed his drink. "I'm going to move over there." He pointed at an empty table next to Maggie's station. "Do you want me to pay up?"

"You can't see the TV from there," said the bartender.

"I'm not watching the TV."

Maggie came around the corner, her face flushed and her eyes sparking with fury. Apparently, his little rabbit didn't like not getting fucked and that was perfect because he'd enjoy taming her temper. She was going to be such a good sub. He hadn't expected her to keep the Ben Wa balls inside her all night. He was a tad disappointed that he wouldn't get to punish her for disobeying but her eagerness to get laid would more than make up for that.

"Oh. Yeah. She's cute but she's got three kids." The bartender handed Terry his bill.

"Don't remind me." He paid and walked to the table, giving her a smirk as he sat.

"What are you doing?" She almost growled.

"Sitting here." This was going to be so much fun.

"You're done eating. Go home."

"I haven't had dessert yet."

"I'll get the waitress." She started to turn away.

"I'll be eating my dessert at home. Tonight. Spread out on the table."

Her body stiffened and he held his breath, wondering if his words had pushed her over the edge into orgasm.

"I'll tell her it's to go." She plastered on her fake hostess smile and left.

A few minutes later the waitress came by and handed him the dessert menu. Maggie walked to her station and began straightening it but she wouldn't look at him .

"What would you recommend?" He opened the menu and shifted it toward the waitress.

"What do you like? Chocolate? Strawberry?" She touched his arm. "Give me a hint. What's your favorite? Pie? Cake?"

"Oh, I'm afraid my favorite isn't on your menu." He glanced at Maggie and her cheeks were red.

"I'm sorry. What is it? Perhaps, I can recommend something similar."

Maggie mumbled something under her breath.

"I'm sorry. Did you suggest something?" He stared at her, struggling to keep from laughing at her look of outrage and embarrassment.

"No, sir." Her face heated even more with that word. She coughed into her hand. "I was just clearing my throat."

"Hmm. Are you sure you don't have a suggestion on which dessert I'd like?"

"I'm sure you'll like them all." She smiled that fake hostess smile again.

"You never did tell me your favorite," said the waitress. "I'm sure we can find something similar."

Maggie made another sound but she quickly hid it with a cough.

"I don't think there's anything like what I eat for dessert on your menu."

"We have a wide selection." The waitress sounded a little annoyed.

"I see that you do, but I don't believe this would be on any menu except perhaps at La Petite Mort Club."

It took a second and then the waitress's eyes widened and she laughed. "Perhaps something with whipped cream." She pointed to a chocolate cake with whipped cream and fudge. "Like this."

"That'll be perfect. Tell them to add extra whipped cream and do you have any fresh cherries?"

"Yes."

"Give me two of those in a separate container. I have special plans for them."

"Sounds fun." The waitress smiled boldly at him.

"It will be." He glanced at Maggie who was still tidying her area, pretending to ignore him. He tossed back his drink and handed it to the waitress. "Another please and make it a double."

"Will do." The waitress took the glass and walked away. She was cute with a nice ass, but he really wasn't into threesomes. Maggie was more than enough for him.

He leaned over by her. "Do you know what I'm going to do with those cherries?"

"No, sir. I have no idea." She kept her face bland and polite as she smiled at him.

He hated that fake smile. He stood and moved closer, probably too close but he wanted her to look at him like she had before, warm and with interest.

She shifted away, glancing down at a paper. "We'll be closing soon. I have a lot of work to get done, so if you don't need me to assist you with anything—"

"But I do, little rabbit," he whispered.

Her eyes darted to his mouth as she shifted to the side, putting her back against the hostess station. "Stop it. I need to get back to work."

His little rabbit was scared. He couldn't wait to show her that she had nothing to fear from being devoured by him. "Good. Hurry up. I'm more than ready to leave and so are you." He let his eyes wander down her frame, lingering on the juncture between her thighs that had to be throbbing for him.

"Not tonight."

"Yes, tonight." He wasn't letting her get away from him now.

"No. I told you this was a one-time thing and—"

He leaned down so only she could hear him. "You are not going home to your vibrator."

"Well, I'm going home alone." She pushed on his chest but he didn't move. "You had your chance and blew it."

"You'll be the one blowing"—he grinned—"but that'll be later."

"Stop it. Enough." Her eyes flashed fire but her voice was low and husky. "I have to finish here and then I'm going home to pack. I don't have time for these games."

"That's exactly why you'll be going home with me." He touched her lips to stop her from talking. "Tomorrow, my friends are coming over and we'll get you packed and moved. I just need to know where you're moving to."

Her anger fled, her gaze softening. "You asked your friends to help me? Why?"

"I knew you didn't want me to pay for movers." He shrugged. He'd show his little rabbit that having him around was a good thing—both in and out of the bedroom.

"That's the sweetest…" She wiped at her eyes.

He kissed her forehead. She deserved someone who'd take care of her. "Get back to work so we can get out of here."

"Thank you." She stared up at him, her eyes huge and teary. "That's the…thank you." She hurried away.

He sat back down and paid his check when the waitress returned. He sipped his drink while waiting for Maggie. Soon she'd realize that he knew best and she should trust him. Then, they could really play.

CHAPTER 13: Maggie

Maggie hurried to finish her work. She was more than eager to show Terry how much she appreciated him. She blinked back tears. Asking his friends to help her pack and move was the nicest thing anyone had ever done for her. She glanced at him as she wrapped silverware in napkins. His eyes were on her and they were narrowed as he sipped his drink.

She smiled but his gaze dropped to her ass. Her hand stilled. He couldn't possibly tell that she'd removed the Ben Wa balls, could he? No, there was no way. She continued preparing the utensils for the next day and he continued to watch her.

Sweat began to trickle down her back. He was going to want to remove them. He'd said so. She'd better put them back for him to find. Her insides clenched with desire and dread. Those things drove her crazy, making her aware of her private parts with every breath and step, but if he discovered that she'd removed them, she'd be punished even more. That thought was like a stroke of his tongue across her pussy. His punishments had been divine so far. She could let him discover…no. He was doing her a huge favor by helping her move. There'd been no way she'd been going to get it done in time by herself. She'd known that, but she'd refused to accept it because that meant hiring movers and she didn't have the money.

Her manager, Mary Lou, walked to Terry's table. "Sir, we're closing now. Would you like us to call you a cab?" She glanced at his glass.

He'd been drinking for hours but he still seemed in control. "Nope. She's my designated driver." He nodded at Maggie.

"Oh. Okay." Mary Lou's eyes dimmed a little. "You'll need to wait outside while we finish."

"Sure." He tossed back his drink and strode to the door.

As soon as he stepped outside, Mary Lou walked over to her. "You're not supposed to have boyfriends here while you work."

Her mouth dropped open. Everyone did it. Max, the bartender, picked up a different woman almost every night and they always sat inside at the bar with him. And Mary Lou's boyfriend had been here every day she closed until they'd broken up. The other woman was just mad because she'd had her eye on Terry all night. She should say something but she'd never liked confrontation. "Okay. I'm sorry." She hated herself for being weak.

"Don't do it again." Mary Lou smiled, but it was catty. "Let's get out of here. I know you have better things to do." She glanced out the door at Terry who was looking at his phone.

"I'm going to use the restroom first. I'll be right back." It was the perfect opportunity to put those things back inside her body. Terry couldn't follow her this time.

When Maggie and the others exited the restaurant, Terry was gone. She looked around the parking lot. He couldn't have left. He wouldn't do that to her. Would he?

A car pulled up and he got out of the driver's side. A surge of relief washed through her. He hadn't left her. It wasn't that she cared. No. This was just a fun fling, but it would've been embarrassing. Everyone knew she was supposed to go home with the hot guy from the bar.

"You drive." He walked to her side and handed her the keys.

"This isn't your car." His was a black Mercedes. This was a Volvo, dark blue and brand new. Now, she remembered. She'd seen it in his garage.

"No, it's yours for as long as you need it." He got into the car.

She stared at his closed door. This was not happening. She walked to the driver's side and got in. "I'm not taking this car." She adjusted the seat, put on her seatbelt and started the engine. It purred, nothing at all like the death rattle she was used to.

"Don't be stupid." He rested his hand on her thigh.

"Not while I'm driving." She moved his hand off her leg. This car was too expensive. If she got in an accident, she'd be indebted to him forever.

"I'm not doing anything." He gently squeezed her thigh. "I missed touching you."

Her heart melted. It'd been a long time since a man had missed anything except her washing his underwear. "Okay, but no funny business." She pulled out of the parking lot and into the street.

"Agreed. Until we get to my house. Then, all bets are off."
He grinned at her in the dark.

He was so darn sexy. Her inner muscles clenched, causing
the toy inside of her to roll. She gasped slightly.

"Like your punishment, don't you?"

She didn't want to answer that. It was embarrassing how
turned on she was. She'd had tampons inside her and they
never, ever made her hot.

"Don't be stubborn, my little rabbit."

"I'm not." She was.

"Then be a good girl and answer my question." His fingers
skimmed back and forth on her leg, right above her knee.

He wasn't anywhere near where she needed him, but even
this small touch was driving her mad and making her so needy
and wet. She shifted on her seat and moaned as the balls rolled,
her muscles clenching around them.

"Pull into that gas station and park on the side."

"Why?" They didn't need gas and she didn't want to delay
getting to his house.

"Because I said so."

"You're not the boss."

"I am. You agreed—"

"That you were the boss when we...you know."

"Trust me and do what I said."

She gave him a dirty look but pulled up by the gas station,
parking on the side of the building. She shouldn't be mad. He
might have to pee. He'd had quite a lot to drink and she could
wait a few more minutes. She didn't want to, but she could.

He leaned over and kissed her ear. "You're so fucking ready

to come, aren't you?"

The breath caught in her throat. She hadn't expected this. "We can't. Not here." Although, she wanted to, needed to.

"We won't." His lips trailed down her neck.

"Then why?" She almost cried. They could've been closer to his house, closer to release.

"We won't but you will." He nipped her ear and his hand skimmed up her leg.

"Here?" She was almost panting. She should stop him, but her legs drifted open.

"No one will even notice." He sat up, moving away from her, except for his hand that crept closer to the juncture between her thighs. "Look at me, like we're talking."

She turned and his eyes sparked with flames of desire. Her gaze dropped to his pants and by the outline in his jeans, he was more than ready. His fingers drifted over her pussy. It was fleeting but every atom in her body zoomed to that spot, tensing for more.

"Look at me. If I can't feel you when you come, I want to at least see you." His voice was rough and she obeyed without thought. "Good girl." He pressed between her legs, his fingers trailing back and forth.

She rolled her hips forward, toward his hand, toward the pleasure. His nostrils flared as he rubbed her. Her hips rocked and the balls inside her shifted. She gasped as he pressed harder.

"You like that, don't you? Those balls rolling around, pressing against you, making you cling to them."

She was panting and thrusting against his hand.

"Answer me."

"Yes." Her eyes drifted half-closed.

"Good girl. Now, I'll reward you." He stopped stroking her.

"Please, Terry. Sir." She almost wept. She'd been so close all night and now to have him stop.

"Shhh." His lips turned up in a smirk but she didn't care because he was unbuttoning her pants.

She wanted to scream "yes" as he pulled down the zipper. She opened her legs wider, watching as his hand disappeared inside her pants.

"Look at me."

She raised her eyes to his.

"Is this what you want?" He rubbed her clit.

"Yes." Her head dropped back against the seat. "God, yes."

He stroked her in long, firm strokes, each movement causing the balls to roll with his rhythm. Her eyes closed and she gasped as the toy bumped against a spot that sent electricity racing through her.

"There, it is." His strokes became shorter and faster, making those balls stay against that spot, rubbing and pressing.

Her fingernails dug into his wrist, holding him against her as waves of pleasure crashed over her. "Oh...oh, Terry." She moaned, her hips jerking against his hand as she came.

"That's it. You were so good tonight." His eyes shimmered in the darkness.

Her heart pounded in her chest but her body felt like her bones had been removed.

His hand slipped from her pants, buttoning and zipping her back up before resting above her knee. "Can you drive?"

"Of course, I can drive." She thought she could anyway.

"Then, let's go."

"We need to go inside and buy something."

"Why? Do you need a drink?"

"No, but you don't stop at a gas station to visit. Even if you only use the restroom, you buy something."

"Why would you do that?"

"Because it's the right thing to do."

"I don't see it."

"If you use their facilities—"

"We didn't. We sat in their parking lot for two minutes while I rubbed you off."

"Don't say it like that." There was no reason for him to be so crass.

He grabbed her chin. "Don't tell me what to do. I'm the boss remember?"

"Only in the bedroom."

"In all sexual encounters."

"That's what I meant."

"That's what this was."

She started the car. "Do you want to leave or not?" The balls shifted, making desire spark to life again. She needed them out and she needed him inside her.

"Not before you submit."

"I just submitted," she said through clenched teeth. She had no idea what he wanted from her. She'd kept those damn things inside her almost all night and then she'd come for him in a parking lot. What kind of woman did those things? She really didn't want to think about that too much.

"Say what I did to you and don't use flowery or evasive words."

"You...you put your hand—"

"Nope. Try again."

The bastard was enjoying this. "You rubbed me."

"And what did you do." This time he couldn't hide his smirk.

"I came."

"Good, rabbit. Now, let's go home so I can fuck you."

CHAPTER 14: Terry

Terry waited for Maggie to chastise him for his language, but she remained silent as she pulled the car out of the parking lot. By the tension in her jaw and the way she was strangling the steering wheel, she was fuming, but like a good sub, she didn't correct or question.

As he leaned back in his seat, his chest puffed out a bit with pride. She wasn't there yet, but she was learning. It'd take time. Her asshole of an ex had annihilated her trusting nature, but he'd show her that trusting the right man was exactly what she needed.

She didn't have to worry about anything but him and his needs. He'd handle everything else. His thoughts screeched to a halt—danger, danger, echoing through his brain. When had this become more than a casual fling?

He glanced at her. She was studying the road, her pique from earlier gone. She was an angel in a siren's body. She gave and forgave so easily. She needed someone to watch out for her and he wanted to be that man. He was in this for the long haul.

He'd spend his time and money to care for her every need. It sounded perfect. Except, as always in life, there were obstacles—namely her three, young kids.

His fingers drummed on his thigh as he stared out the window. Her ex took the children on a bi-weekly basis, so he could see her then. Plus, there was school, day care and summer camp. He usually didn't bother working around a woman's schedule but Maggie was different. The more he fucked her the more he wanted.

She'd have to quit her job so she could be there when he wanted her, except if the kids needed her, of course. Even he wasn't a big enough ass to try and make her choose him over her children. Kids always came first and then she could take care of him.

She turned into his driveway. He pressed the button on his phone that opened the garage. She pulled the car inside and turned it off, shifting slightly on the seat. The Ben Wa balls were still working their magic. He couldn't wait to fuck her, but he was going to because teasing her with that toy came first.

He got out of the car.

"Don't forget your dessert." She stepped out of the car, holding the bag from the restaurant.

"Oh, don't worry. I'll have my dessert." He let his eyes drift over her breasts and down to the juncture of her thighs.

"That's not what I meant."

"I'm sure." He held the door open. "Now, hurry up."

She moved past him and he followed her into the house. She stopped and petted Beast who greeted them at the door.

"Hey, boy." He patted the dog. "You hungry? Gotta go out?"

Beast hurried to the back door, tail wagging.

"Go ahead and put the dessert in the refrigerator." Terry followed his dog, opening the sliding glass door to his back yard. "This will only take a minute."

Beast darted outside and Terry walked into the kitchen as Maggie was closing the refrigerator.

He moved behind her and pulled her against him. "Do you feel what you do to me?" He rubbed his erection against her ass, his hands cupping her breasts while he nibbled her neck. "All night long, I watched you. Wanting to touch but I couldn't." She melted against him and he got harder. Fuck, he was going to come in his pants. "You're going to pay for that."

"I was at work. It wasn't my fault."

"Don't care." He nipped her ear and teased her neck with his teeth and tongue as his fingers plucked at her nipples through her blouse. "You'll pay"—he stepped away, smirking at her slight moan of protest—"as soon as I take care of Beast."

He turned and opened a kitchen cabinet pulling out a can of wet dog food. "Go into the living room. Take off your shoes, socks, shirt and bra and get down on your knees in front of my chair."

She spun around, mouth partway open like she was ready to argue. He held his breath, waiting to see if she'd obey. Her eyes sparked a little and he couldn't tell if it was irritation or desire, but she started unbuttoning her shirt and he leaned against the counter to watch. Beast could wait a minute.

She stared at him as her fingers made their way down her blouse, exposing all that warm, soft flesh. He rested his hand on his dick. It was going to explode if he didn't give it some attention. Her eyes dropped to his pants and she licked her lips.

It was just a small darting of her tongue, unintentional and all the more erotic because of it.

His dick grew against his hand, demanding that it come out and meet that luscious tongue. "You're playing with fire, little rabbit."

She smiled and removed her shirt. "And I believe you have the hose to take care of that."

He laughed. This was the first time she'd been playful. That meant she was getting more comfortable with him and their roles. "Oh, I have the hose all right and I'm going to show it to you."

"All I get to do is look?" She reached behind her to the clasp of her bra.

"No. Tonight, you'll get to taste it, among other things." His eyes fastened on her chest. He needed to see her tits. He was pretty sure he'd die if he didn't.

"Then hurry up and take care of your dog." The bra loosened but she held the front against her chest so it wouldn't fall. "I'll be on my knees waiting." She turned and sauntered into the living room.

She had to feel the Ben Wa balls rolling with each step. There was no way she wasn't as turned on as he was. He hurried to the door and let Beast in. The dog ran right to his dish.

"You ready for your special treat?" he asked the dog.

Beast barked.

He pulled the lid off the can. "I know, I am."

Maggie laughed from the living room.

He tipped the can, dropping the contents onto the dry dog food still in the dish. As soon as he moved his hand, Beast lowered his head and began eating. The dog had enough water, so his duties were done. He tossed the can in the garbage and washed his hands. The only flavor he wanted on his fingers was pussy.

He strode into the living room, kicking off his shoes as he went. He stopped to take in the picture. Maggie knelt on a pillow that she'd put on the floor in front of his chair, wearing just her pants. Her breasts were bare and magnificent.

"What a good rabbit." He walked across the room to stand in front of her. Her eyes were about eye level with his crotch. "You know what I want."

"Yes, Sir. I was waiting for your command."

He stroked her hair, loosening the bun and letting the dark strands cascade around her shoulders. "That's a good girl. Now, take out my dick and suck it."

CHAPTER 15: Maggie

Maggie reached up, eager to take Terry's cock out of his pants and play with it. She'd never been a fan of blow jobs with David, but this…this was different. David had always been almost apologetic about it, like it was wrong or dirty somehow. Terry wasn't apologetic at all. He stared down at her, his eyes dark and hooded, waiting patiently, expectantly. This would please him and that made her happy.

She unhooked his button and slowly unzipped his pants, letting the tension build as he stroked her hair. She could smell his musk and it made her wetter. She leaned forward and kissed him through his underwear.

"That's it." His hand continued to play with her hair, but it was also edging her forward. He was quite eager and so was she.

She shoved his pants down but left his underwear. She ran her fingers up and down his cock. He was so big—both long and thick, like a delicious, hot popsicle—that she'd never get that entire thing in her mouth. She'd have to focus on the tip and use her hands for the rest.

"Maggie…" The word was a groan. "No playing. Not right now. Take it out and suck it."

"Yes, Sir." She grinned up at him as she pulled his underwear down and his dick bobbed in front of her. "It's…ah…bigger than I remember." Now, she wasn't so sure about this. That thing was a monster, waving in front of her face.

CHAPTER 16: Terry

Terry couldn't wait any longer to feel Maggie's mouth around his dick. He'd been on edge all night and it was time to relieve some pressure. "Open." He grabbed his cock and ran it over her lips. They were warm and soft and he had to get inside all that wet heat.

She stared at his dick like she'd never seen one before.

It was time to assure her, build her confidence, but all he wanted to do was fuck her face. His breath rattled in his chest as he wrangled his desire under control. "You can do this." He stroked her cheek.

She nodded, eyes still affixed to his throbbing cock. Her tongue darted out, sliding across his tip.

Fuck, it felt good. "That's it, baby. Keep going."

She wrapped her hand around his dick. He bit back a groan as she squeezed. He dropped his arms to his sides so she could set the pace. Her hand stroked him as she licked all around the tip, letting her tongue play along the slit.

"Suck it, Maggie." He couldn't take the teasing anymore.

He clasped her head, holding her in place. "Now." He almost begged.

Her eyes locked with his. She was enjoying the power she had and he was glad because that meant she'd want to do this again. Lord knows, he was willing. She opened wide and he slid his dick past her lips. The warmth and heat of her mouth almost made his knees buckle. He was so hard. This wouldn't take long. She sucked at the tip and his eyes fluttered half-shut. She began working her hand up and down his shaft.

"That's it. Take more, baby. For me." He needed to be deeper inside her. He thrust forward.

She gagged.

He pulled back a little. "Breath through your nose. You can do this."

She opened wider and he slid farther into her mouth. Her tongue played along his dick as she sucked and stroked.

"That's it. That's my girl." It was heaven—hot, wet heaven—and he couldn't stop his hips from thrusting. "God, your mouth feels so fucking good."

Her head bobbed, following his rhythm as her other hand played with his balls.

"Fuck. Yes." He pumped faster but he let go of her head, tangling his hands in her hair. "Keep going. I'm not gonna last long."

She pulled off him with a pop.

His jaw tensed as his hand cupped the back of her neck. This was not the time to stop or to tease. "Finish, Maggie."

"Don't you want—"

"I'm going to come in your mouth and you're going to swallow every bit."

"Ah…" By the look on her face this was new to her.

His hand trembled as he stroked her cheek. "If you don't like it, we never have to do it again." But he really wanted to feel her suck him as he came, feel her mouth squeezing his dick as she swallowed.

"I've done it before and didn't like it."

"But you never did it with me." His thumb ran across her lips, slipping into her mouth. Her tongue darted out, tasting his skin.

"That's it, baby."

She wrapped her lips around his thumb and sucked. His nostrils flared and his dick jumped. She was ready.

"For me. Do it for me." He pulled his thumb out and grabbed his dick, positioning it at her mouth. "Open."

She did. His perfect sub, his little rabbit, obeyed. His cock slid back inside her mouth and she sucked, running her tongue along his skin while her hands worked his shaft and balls.

"That's it. Yes." The pleasure was roaring through him. His hips moved faster in short jabs, so not to gag her. She wasn't ready for deep throating him, not yet. "Fuck."

He was so close—the tightness, the suction making his balls harden. His hands tangled in her hair, holding her in place as she sucked harder and stroked faster. The hand on his balls left. He forced himself to focus. She was rubbing her pussy, faster and faster, her breasts swaying, her face flushed. It was so hot, he almost blew right then, but instead he yanked on her hair.

"Stop touching yourself." He panted. "Only I touch that pussy."

Her hand froze as her eyes went back to his.

"Did…I…give you…permission to come?" He kept thrusting

into her mouth even though she wasn't sucking any longer.

She started to pull off him, but he held her in place.

"You know your safeword. Do you need to use it?" He'd die if she did. He'd drop to his knees and keel over from lust.

She shook her head, her mouth still around his dick. Her hand moved from between her legs to his balls and she started sucking again.

"That's it, baby." Relief and pleasure surged through him. She wasn't going to stop.

She flicked him with her tongue at the same time she squeezed his balls and then sucked.

"Fuck. Yes." He grasped her face, holding her still as he thrust into her mouth and came.

CHAPTER 17: Maggie

Maggie had to swallow. There really was no other choice. Terry's hands held her head as his cock spurted inside her. She swallowed and it was warm and strong but not unpleasant.

He moaned. "Fuck, baby. Yes." His grip loosened and he stroked her hair as he pulled from her mouth. He stared down at her, his eyes warm and dark as he ran his thumb over her chin, catching a string of semen. "Open."

She did, sucking his cum from his finger. She'd always been an obedient person but this man could make her do anything and enjoy it. She'd never been turned on by giving David head, but with Terry it was different. He was so in control, so in charge except when her lips were around his cock. Then, the power had been hers and it'd been an aphrodisiac.

"That's my girl." He took her hand and helped her stand. He bent and kissed her, his tongue darting into her mouth.

After a blow job, David would never kiss her until she brushed her teeth, but Terry's tongue explored her mouth, while one of his hands played with her ass and the other her nipple.

She wrapped her arms around his neck, rubbing herself against him like a cat wanting attention. She was on edge and ready to go.

He broke the kiss and bent, pulling up his underwear and pants.

"You're getting dressed?" That was not what she wanted. Not at all.

He grabbed her chin and kissed her. It was quick and hard. "Trust me."

"Okay." She frowned. She was so horny he'd better not plan on keeping that cock in his pants for long.

"Now, it's my turn." He took her hand and led her into the kitchen.

David had liked to eat or sleep after sex. She wasn't ready to do either. If she said something, he might punish her and although his punishments were lovely, she needed this last one done. The balls shifted and wiggled with each step and they'd rocked inside her while she'd been giving him head. She bit her lip to keep quiet.

"Only I get to do that." He kissed her, pulling her close.

She almost moaned as her nipples, already hard and eager, rubbed against his shirt. He grabbed her and lifted her, sitting her on the table. As soon as she was down, his hands cupped her breasts, tweaking her nipples as he left hot, wet kisses down her chest.

Her head dropped back, her fingers tangling in his hair as he teased along her skin, kissing everywhere but her nipples. She tried to pull him closer, to direct his lips, but he stayed where he was, only a whisper from her tiny buds, letting his breath fan over them. She shifted, her nipple brushing against his face but he lifted away, a teasing glint in his eyes as they locked with hers. His hands skimmed down her body in a slow caress to her waist. He leaned forward and licked one nipple, rubbing the tip around his tongue like a berry. The rough heat sent shivers to her pussy, making her throb. She wrapped her legs around his waist, dragging him closer.

"God, you're so fucking hot." His lips clamped down around her nipple, sucking and laving it with his tongue.

"Oh, yes. Please." She needed this and so much more. She was so on edge, so close. She grabbed one of his hands and put it on her upper thigh. She needed him to touch her there too.

"Not yet, rabbit." He bit down on her nipple.

The slight pain from his teeth mixed with the pleasure, sending her over the edge. She moaned, her body shaking with her release.

"Fuck. I didn't expect that." His hand moved between her thighs, rubbing in firm, fast strokes.

The balls rocked within her as another wave of pleasure shot through her body. She trembled, her nails digging into his shoulders and her hips thrusting greedily against his hand, searching for every last bit of pleasure.

"That's it." He whispered against the side of her head, his hand slowing between her legs until it was nothing more than lovely pressure. "You did it again."

"What?" She forced her eyes open.

"Fuck," he said under his breath. "You're so fucking gorgeous when you come." He kissed her. It was hard and fast. "I should punish you for coming again without my permission but all I want to do right now is fuck you so hard that you

71

scream."

"Okay by me." Actually, that sounded like a fabulous idea. She grabbed the waistband of his pants, unhooking the button and moving to the zipper.

"Not so fast." He caught her wrists.

"What?" She dragged her eyes away from the bulge in his pants—that lovely, large and delicious bulge was back and ready to play.

"If my cock comes out, it's over. I'll have your legs in the air and be fucking you before you can blink."

"And that's a problem?" She flushed at her boldness. She'd never been like this but she wanted him now.

He kissed her nose. "I still haven't had my dessert."

"What dessert? Oh." She was pretty sure he didn't mean the chocolate cake. She was sitting on his kitchen table. Her face hot from embarrassment and anticipation.

His fingers slipped under her waistband, teasing the soft skin of her belly. Her eyelids lowered. *Yes, remove the clothes. Mine and yours.*

"Those balls inside you are nice, aren't they?"

"Yes," she sighed. "And no."

"Oh, you'll love them soon." He unfastened her pants before grabbing her ass and lifting her from the table.

She helped him tug her pants and underwear down, kicking them off her feet as she ran her hands along his chest, pushing up his shirt. "This needs to go."

"Will that make you happy?"

"Yes." It was a start.

"Then by all means." His eyes heated as he pulled off his shirt.

That gorgeous, hot, male body in front of her was all hers. She leaned forward, kissing her way across his chest. It was payback time. Her tongue darted all around his nipple before she sucked, letting her teeth scrape him gently.

He tugged her hair. "Enough. This is my turn. Remember?"

She smiled. "Of course, Sir. Whatever you want."

"Don't say that if you don't mean it." He grabbed her chin. "Did you mean it?"

"I-I'm not sure." There were a lot of things she didn't want to do, but she would've said that exact thing about swallowing and she'd enjoyed doing that for him.

"Don't say it again unless you are."

"O-okay." Was she ready to let him do anything to her...with her?

"Now, lie back but stay on your elbows."

Her mind tumbled over all the things she'd heard about doms and subs—tying up, whipping—as she stretched out on the table.

He grabbed one of her legs and lifted it, kissing her inner thigh. Her mind screeched to a halt, all her focus on him. He placed her foot on the table and repeated the process with the other one.

She was naked and splayed out like a Christmas turkey. Her breath came in shallow pants as her heart raced, waiting for what he'd do next.

"You're so fucking beautiful." He caressed her soft, rounded tummy.

She hadn't expected the insult. She turned her head.

"Look at me." He leaned forward, grabbing her chin.

She tried, but she couldn't meet his gaze. She was fat and

soft.

"You are beautiful."

"Please, stop saying that."

He slapped her on the side of her ass.

"Hey." That'd been unexpected and it'd hurt, kind of. It'd also sent a jolt of desire between her thighs.

"I'm in charge, right?" His hand caressed where he'd hit her, easing the sting.

"Yes." She'd agreed to that, but it was fleeting. Only a few nights. No, just tonight. This weekend and then it'd be over.

"But?"

"Nothing." She wasn't going into this with him.

"Tell me." He stared at her but she just shook her head. "Oh rabbit, you have to learn to trust me for this to be really good."

"I do trust you."

"Not enough for what I want to do to you."

Her eyes locked with his as the throbbing between her legs revved up a notch or ten. "What more do you want to do?"

"Lots." He kissed her, sinking his tongue into her heat before pulling away. "Now, don't interrupt me again or you'll wear these"—his hand tugged gently on the string between her legs—"all day tomorrow while we pack and move. My friends will be there with their girlfriends and they'll recognize that look of heated lust on your face."

"Your friends have girlfriends?"

"Why is that so surprising?"

"It isn't. It's just...you belong to a sex club," she whispered the last two words.

"Yeah, and they met their girlfriends there. One is even a

fiancé." His lips curled with distaste.

"You don't like her?"

"She's fine."

"You don't like marriage."

"Not particularly. My business has branched out, but I built my practice as a divorce lawyer."

"Oh." A small, stupid part of her that she hadn't even been aware existed, died. This was a fling. That was all. They'd both been clear on that, but a secret part of her had wanted more.

"Enough talking. I'd be laughed out of the Club if anyone found out we'd been having a conversation while I had you naked on my table."

"Blackmail time." She grinned.

"Nope. It's time for my dessert."

Her entire body tensed and tingled with anticipation as he lowered his mouth to hers. This time he grabbed her head, tipping it and giving his tongue better access as he thrust into her mouth. She wanted to wrap her arms around him, but she was balanced on her elbows so she settled for matching his kiss stroke for stroke. He tightened his grip on her head, ravaging her mouth like he was going to ravage her body and she melted at the onslaught. They may not have forever, but they had tonight and she was going to make every minute count.

He broke the kiss and straightened, pulling up a chair. "Now, for dessert."

His dark eyes raked over her body, settling between her thighs. Her face was on fire as she lay like a feast before him, open and ripe, waiting for him to taste and tease. He leaned forward, trailing hot, wet kisses up her thigh.

She was so ready, her juices leaked down her legs and

more flowed as he nuzzled her pussy.

"You taste fantastic," he whispered against her thigh.

She whimpered as his hands pushed her legs farther apart.

"I can't wait any longer." He lowered his mouth, his tongue dipping inside before licking along her sides in long, slow caresses.

"Oh..." The heat and roughness of his tongue made her body hum. How had she'd gone all these years without this? She dropped back onto the table, her hands clasping his hair and pulling him closer.

He licked faster, his tongue dipping inside her and then stroking along her clit.

"Oh...yes." Her body arched into his face as he flicked her sensitive nub while rubbing his fingers against her pussy, making the toy inside her jiggle and jump. Her thighs tightened, squeezing him. She was so close. She just needed a little more.

His hand slowed as he lifted his face. "I told you to watch me."

"What?" She raised her head. Why had he stopped? He couldn't be done, not yet.

"On your elbows." He gave her pussy a quick slap.

"Oh..." Her body twitched. That'd felt so good. The slight sting, right there. She'd never thought...

"Up on your elbows and watch me eat you out."

"Please, Ter...Sir. I can't. It's too much." She'd come if she had to watch.

"On your elbows or I stop."

She closed her eyes, praying for the strength to hold back her orgasm as she leaned up on her elbows.

He grabbed her neck, gently caressing her throat with his

thumb. "I'm going to buy you a collar." He began palming her pussy again. "You'd be so beautiful. You'd belong to me."

A collar. She didn't want to wear a collar.

"I'd make you watch. Hold the leash, force you to look at me."

The image was imprinted in her mind—her naked like this, him between her thighs, holding a lead to keep her head up. She'd have no control. He'd command her as his tongue did lovely things to her body. Tension pooled between her legs. She was going to come. She closed her eyes, trying to keep the passion at bay.

"Look at me or I'm going to have to punish you." With that he thrust a finger inside of her, stroking along the Ben Wa balls.

Her eyes flew open and her face tightened as sensation zipped through her body. She couldn't hold out much longer.

"Ask me before you come." He rolled the balls again.

"Please, Sir. I need to come."

He nipped her right where her thigh met her pussy.

She gasped, her body tightening and clenching around him.

"Don't tell me what you need. Ask me if you can come and you'd better beg because you're pissing me off."

CHAPTER 18: Maggie

Maggie was going to die. She was literally going to burst into sparks if she didn't come. "Please. Sir. May I come? Please." The last word was a moan of anguish and desperation.

His eyes gleamed as he rubbed that long finger inside her, making the toy roll against her g-spot. Her thighs trembled, shaking the table.

She had to convince him. "I was good. I kept this in…" She clamped down on her bottom lip as he continued to stroke her.

"That's true. Although, you were going to take them out."

"But I didn't." She rocked her hips, trying to persuade him to move faster and harder. He was keeping her dancing on the edge of the cliff and she wanted to jump off and fly.

"Didn't you?" He raised a brow. "Even later, after I left you hot and horny in the bathroom. Unfulfilled."

Her eyes locked with his. She'd never been a good liar.

"Tell me the truth." He lowered his head and ran his tongue along her slit, stopping right below her clit.

"Oh…god…please, Sir. May I come. Please." Her whole

body was tense and trembling.

"The truth and you can come."

"Yes. I took them out but I put them back."

"When?"

"Right after I forgave you. Please." Her muscles clamped down on his fingers. She was so close.

He continued to stroke her in that slow, steady pace. "I'm glad you told me the truth, but you will need to be punished for your disobedience." His eyes were dark with dangerous promise. "Understand?"

"Yes. Yes, Sir. Please." She didn't care what he did to her later. Nothing mattered but this moment.

"You may come." He thrust another finger inside her, rolling the toy against her g-spot as he stroked faster and harder.

She was spiraling out of control and she lost it when his dark head lowered, his eyes still locked with hers as he sucked her clit. Her body bucked and tightened, squeezing him but he kept sucking and stroking. She screamed as an orgasm ripped through her. She dropped back onto the table. Her arms too weak to hold herself up any longer. He gave her pussy one last kiss and removed his fingers.

"I think we're done with this"—he pulled the toy from her body—"for tonight." He stared at her as he put them in his mouth, cleaning them off.

She moaned, both wanting and dreading the next time he used them. He stood and tossed them into the sink before opening the fridge. He came back with the dessert bag and a fork. She started to sit up.

"Where do you think you're going?" He put his hand on her

abdomen, keeping her in place.

"I thought you were going to eat." She looked at the dessert bag. "I'm on the table." Nothing was making sense in her ecstasy fogged brain.

"I am, but I'm not done with you yet. However"—he grabbed her hand—"you're right. You should sit up." He tugged and used his other hand to steady her as she sat up on the table, her bones still mush from her last orgasm. "Do you need some water or something else to drink?"

He stared at her with such concern and care she wanted to cry. She didn't remember David ever looking at her like that. Terry tormented her and demanded she bend to his will but he was also so caring. He bent, his lips meeting hers. His tongue dipped into her mouth, slow and sensual. She could taste herself and it was erotic.

He pulled back. "How about some water?"

She nodded, still unable to talk because if she did her voice would crack. He'd realize she was about to cry for absolutely no good reason. She used the few seconds while he went to the counter to wipe her eyes and pull herself together. This man wasn't for her long term. This was a weekend fling. As soon as her kids came home, it was over. She'd go back to her day-to-day struggles of her new life as a poor single mother.

He came back and handed her a glass. "Drink."

She did, gulping it down. She was thirstier than she'd thought.

"Better?"

"Yes. Thank you." She looked up at him through her lashes. "You always know exactly what I need, Sir." She liked playing with him. It made her happy to make him happy.

"Remember that." He took the glass and put it on the counter before sitting down. "Now, to finish my dessert."

He opened the bag and pulled out the two containers, opening one of them. The white whipped cream accentuated the rich dark chocolate of the cake and the frosting. Her mouth watered. She hoped he was going to share. She was starving. She hadn't had time for a break because they'd been so busy. All she'd had was a handful of pretzels from a bag in the back.

"This looks delicious. Lots of whipped cream and"—he picked up the other container—"two cherries for later."

He must really like cherries. She'd have to bake him a cherry pie. No, this was over after this weekend, but David was going to take the kids again the weekend after next. If she timed her delivery of the "thank you pie" right, she might get another weekend of forgetting about her life and just being a woman desired by him.

He stood and put the container with the cherries in the freezer and sat down, breaking off a piece of the cake with the fork. "Open."

He held it to her lips and she gladly accepted it. Her eyes closed as the sugary goodness melted on her tongue.

"Like that, do you?"

"Yes, Sir." She smiled and took the next bite he offered. "It's delicious."

"Can't be as delicious as you." He gave her another piece.

She felt her cheeks heat. David hadn't liked going down on her. He'd done it a few times but always hurried right to the bathroom to brush his teeth and gargle. She'd understood, but he certainly didn't want her to do that after she gave him a blow job. Sometimes, she'd swear he choose those nights to snuggle so that she couldn't brush her teeth.

She ate another piece of cake. With Terry, she was in no hurry to wash the taste of him from her mouth. The cake was covering it now, but the dark, male musk still lingered on the back of her tongue and she liked it.

"Do you want some more water?" He asked as he fed her another piece of cake.

"Aren't you going to have any?" He'd given her almost all his dessert.

"I saved some for me." He offered her the second to last piece.

"You only want one bite?" That was crazy. "This is really good."

"There's more than enough left for me." He held the last piece up to her lips. "Open."

She did, obeying like she had when she'd been on her knees. Both times it was delicious.

He turned and tossed the fork into the sink. "Now, my turn."

"But there's nothing left." She was starting to feel bad about this.

"There's plenty." He scooped up a glob of whipped cream and some of the chocolate syrup on his finger.

She gasped as he plopped it on her nipple. He scraped more and decorated her other nipple before running his finger down her torso. He grabbed more dessert and painted over her hip bones on each side, down her inner thigh and the outer sides of her pussy.

He slowly licked his fingers, his eyes locking with hers. She shivered, knowing where that mouth would be soon. He bent his head and licked her nipple.

"You're right. It is delicious." His tongue was rough as it lapped up the whipped cream, going around and around her areola.

"Yes." One of her hands clutched his broad shoulder, loving the play of muscles under her fingers, but her other hand tangled in his soft hair, holding him closer. She'd never tire of the feelings he created in her. It was like a whirlpool—sex, desire, caring, commands and laughter all swirling inside her making her feel safe.

CHAPTER 19: Terry

Terry couldn't get enough of Maggie. She was sweeter than the dessert, but it was pretty damn good. He kissed his way across her chest. This time he didn't tease but latched right onto her nipple, sucking all that rich cream and dark chocolate. Her little mews of pleasure and her hand stroking his hair had him ready to burst but he'd wait. It was better that way and she was going to wait this time too. His hand drifted between her legs, skimming through her lower lips and teasing her hard, little nub. Her legs clasped around his sides.

He lifted his head. She was like the poster girl for sex and seduction. Her eyes were closed and her face was tight with pleasure. Her hair tumbled around her shoulders and her nipples were red and glistening from his mouth.

He took a deep, shaky breath. "Open your ey..." He groaned as she opened her mouth. He couldn't help it. He had to do it. His finger dipped into her pussy, careful not to get any of the dessert inside of her, and then between her lips. She sucked and he swore he felt it in his balls.

Her eyes fluttered opened, a look of surprise swirling in the passion.

"I told you that you tasted delicious." His dick twitched when she sucked harder. He pulled his finger from her mouth. "Pay attention." Her eyes locked with his as her hand continued to stroke his hair. "You are not to come until I tell you."

"But..."

"No excuses." He pinched her nipple.

She gasped, her eyes shuttering half-closed.

"Understand?"

"Yes."

"Yes, what?"

"Yes, Sir." She sighed the last word, her hand pressing his head downward.

He should correct her for trying to persuade him to get back to it, but since that was what he wanted too, there was no point. Plus, he could punish her later for it, after they'd both come and rested. He lowered his face and kissed his way down her body, following the chocolate and cream. Her skin was warm and salty, mixing beautifully with the dessert.

Her legs fell open as he neared. She was so hot for him. He breathed over her pussy, her musky arousal making his dick scream in protest for still being locked in his pants. Her body tensed, waiting for his touch but he moved his face, kissing over to her hip and following his line of chocolate. She whimpered, her fingers tugging on his hair. He smiled against her leg.

"Patience, sweet." He kissed his way back up to her abdomen and over to her other hip. Her body arched toward him. He licked her stomach and lower.

"Please, Sir." She thrust upward toward his face.

"You can't come." He spread her lower lips, relishing the slick wetness that glistened, calling to him. "So, fucking beautiful." He couldn't wait any longer. His tongue came out, tasting her—one side and then the other. Her flavor mixed with the cream and chocolate and he moaned. "They should bottle this. I'd fucking eat it every day."

"Yes." Now, both her hands grasped his head, trying to pull him back against her.

"Yes? I'll hold you to that. I get to eat your pussy every day."

"Hmm." She yanked on his hair. "Please, Terr...Sir."

He licked her again and she trembled. He let his tongue lay flat against her clit. Her body trembled.

"Do not come." He lifted off her but couldn't force himself to move away. He breathed her in as his hand caressed her thigh in soft strokes. "Tell me when I can continue."

"Please." She rocked her hips toward his face. "Now. Please, Sir."

"Tell me when you aren't on the edge. When you won't come."

"Oh." She sounded so depressed.

He'd laugh if he wasn't so fucking close to the edge himself.

She took several deep breaths and he stared at her cunt, glistening and swollen for him. God, he needed to taste that. Needed to fuck that.

"Okay. You can continue." Her breath was shaky but in control.

He didn't need to hear it twice. He walked to the fridge and grabbed the cherries from the freezer. He put the container on the table. "Watch me."

He placed one of the cold cherries over her clit.

"That's freezing," she gasped, bucking under his hand.

"And this is hot." He covered the fruit with his mouth, alternating sucking her clit and rolling the cherry over the sensitive nub.

"Oh...god." Her fingers dug into his scalp, holding him in place.

He continued to lick her until the cherry warmed. He leaned up. She was staring at him, her eyes dark with passion and her face flushed. He showed her the cherry between his teeth. She shivered as he bit down on it, the juices coating his teeth and tongue. "More." He tossed the stem and seed aside. "But this one goes inside."

"I don't know about—"

"Trust me." He dangled it by the stem. "I promise not to lose it. May I?"

She nodded. "Yes, Sir."

His gaze locked with hers as he placed the fruit inside her body. She shivered. "Want me to warm it?"

She licked her lips. "Yes, Sir. Please."

He lowered his head and licked her again. She was so fucking sweet. He probed her with his tongue, thrusting around the cherry and then pulled it out. He leaned up. She was still watching him, this time her lips were open and her breath was coming in pants.

He removed the stem and seed before putting the cherry between his teeth and dipping his head to slip the fruit into her mouth. He pulled back, watching as she chewed. "How is it?"

"Delicious." She licked her lips and his control snapped.

His mouth came down on hers, ravaging as he yanked open his pants. "I'm going to fuck you now," he said against her lips.

"Yes. May I come?"

"As many times as you like." He straightened, grabbed a condom from his wallet and shoved down his pants. He tore the packet open and covered his cock. This was going to stop. He wanted to be inside her bare—raw, just her and him—but they'd talk about that later. He grabbed her thighs and yanked her toward him, until her ass was half-off the table.

"Now, Maggie." It was part question and part command.

"Yes, please, Sir. Now." Her breathing was rapid and her body tense.

He grabbed his dick and thrust into her as he pulled her toward him. She gasped and he moaned. She was so fucking tight and hot and wet and everything he'd ever wanted. His hips moved fast and hard. He was beyond slow and controlled.

She screamed and her body bucked against him as she came. He kept pumping into her over and over. She struggled under him, as if trying to get away but his hands clamped onto her ass, tipping her up and holding her close. She moaned again as her body shook with her second orgasm. This one latched onto his dick so hard it almost hurt. He shoved into her again and it was done. His body tensed, succumbing to his own release.

CHAPTER 20: Maggie

Maggie was boneless. She had no idea how long she'd lain on the table with Terry draped over her, but her breathing was back to normal and she could move again. Not that she wanted to. She'd be happy staying here with him surrounding her and inside her, the scent of sex and chocolate in the air. She should be blushing at what they'd done but she didn't feel one iota of shame or embarrassment. She skimmed her nails gently up and down his back.

"Mmm. That feels great." He kissed her neck where his face was buried.

"You feel great." She kissed the side of his head.

"Keep this up and we'll be fucking again."

"Fine with me, Sir." She wrapped her legs around him.

He chuckled but straightened, pulling out of her. "I'd love to but I don't know if your back could take another round on the table." He grabbed her hands and pulled her to a sitting position.

His dark eyes roamed her body. She straightened her

shoulders, causing her breasts to push out a bit. His eyes sparkled. She was still a little embarrassed about the extra weight but he didn't seem to mind.

"Come." He took her hand and helped her off the table. Her legs wobbled and he bent, picking her up.

"Put me down. I'm too heavy."

"Not at all and I'm the boss. Remember?" He tossed her in the air and she squealed, wrapping her arms around his neck as he walked. "That's better, rabbit." He stopped in his bedroom, letting her slide down his body to the floor. "Stay right there." He disappeared in the bathroom.

Now that he was gone, she was self-conscious standing in the nude. Her butt and thighs were too big and she had puckers of cellulite in the largest areas. Her breasts weren't nearly as firm as before she'd had the kids. That's it. She was covering up with something. One of his T-shirts hung over the back of a chair. She grabbed it and put it on. There was the sound of water running. The shower was hers next. She was still sticky from the chocolate and cream, not that he'd left much.

He came out of the bathroom and stopped. "I told you to stay."

"I did." She was still in the room.

"You weren't wearing my clothes when I left." His eyes were stern but amusement sparkled in their dark depths along with a heat that made her shiver.

"I-I..." She wasn't sure what to say. I felt embarrassed standing here naked after you went down on me and fed me a cherry from between my legs, seemed kind of stupid.

He strode over to her and grabbed the bottom of his shirt. She raised her arms and he smiled. "So naturally obedient, but that brain of yours keeps getting in the way." He pulled the shirt off and tossed it aside. He cupped her chin. "Now, listen closely. I like your body. I like looking at it. I like touching it." His voice lowered and his eyes darkened. "I certainly like tasting it and fucking it."

"But I'm fat." She couldn't stop the words. David had told her numerous times to lose weight. He'd blamed her extra pounds on their lack of a sex life more than once. Before she could say anything else, Terry's hand landed on her ass. "Ouch." She jumped.

"Don't ever call yourself that again."

"That stung." She rubbed her butt.

"Good. Maybe, you'll remember. I'm the boss and if I say you're beautiful, you are beautiful."

Her heart melted a little but her insecurity struggled to the surface. "I'm glad you think so—"

He hit her butt again. "I don't *think* so. You are."

She frowned, not sure if she was enjoying this or not. He yanked her against him, his hand caressing where he'd spanked her. Okay, now she was enjoying it.

"You are beautiful." He kissed her, his mouth taking and invading, leaving her no room for thought.

"Say it," he said against her lips.

"Yes, Sir."

He grinned. "No. Say you're beautiful."

"You're—"

"Don't be a smart ass." He swatted her again, but this time his hand lingered, teasing between her crack. "Say it." He kissed her. "For me."

Right now, she'd do anything for him. "I'm beautiful."

"I'm going to make you say it until you believe it."

"We'll be at this a long time." She wrapped her arms around his neck, pinpricks of passion stirring to life as her breasts rubbed against his chest.

"Come." He lifted her, his hands under her ass, and carried her into the shower. "Get in. You're all sticky."

She stepped into the steaming, hot shower and Terry followed behind her, his large body filling the stall. He grabbed the shampoo and positioned her so she was facing away from him, her head under the water. He began washing her hair, his strong hands massaging her scalp.

"Oh, that feels so good." She almost melted into a puddle at his feet when his began rubbing her neck and shoulders. "Keep doing that and I'll be your slave."

"That's the plan." He adjusted the spray nozzle and rinsed the soap from her hair. Then his hands were back and he was massaging conditioner into her scalp.

She almost whimpered when he finished with her hair but was saved when he grabbed a washcloth and began washing her body, his touch lingering on her breasts.

"Gotta clean these good. They had a lot of dessert on them." His voice was a rough whisper in her ear.

"Yes." She arched her back, pushing her breasts into his hands, loving the feel of the fabric rubbing her body.

He tweaked her nipples as his other hand, sans washcloth, dipped between her legs. "Here too."

"I'm very dirty there." She tipped her head, kissing him.

"Then I need to give it special attention." His finger played around her clit.

She moaned, wrapping her arms around his neck. This man

was magic. She'd just been exhausted and now she was raring to go another round. She rubbed her ass against him and was a little disappointed that he wasn't hard.

"Don't worry, rabbit. I'll be ready to go soon. I need a little more time than you to rev up."

"Oh, no." She'd hurt his feelings. David would've been storming away by now. "It's fine."

He nipped her ear. "I know it is. Now, relax and let me take care of you." He thrust two fingers inside her and his other hand, pressed down on her abdomen as he stroked in and out.

"Oh...oh..." She had no idea what he was doing but when he curled his fingers and pressed his other hand against her abdomen, the pleasure was so pure and intense that she shattered, hard and fast, trembling in his arms.

His caresses slowed as her shaking subsided. He kissed her neck. "Hold still." He removed his hand from between her legs and began washing himself.

She turned. "Let me." She reached up and he ducked his head so she could wash his hair.

His hair was thick and dark between her fingers but too soon she was done. She grabbed the washcloth and covered it with soap. She ran it up and over his chest and arms. She loved men's bodies. They were so strong and dependable, especially Terry. For a guy in his forties, he was all muscle. "You must work out all the time." Her hand trailed around to his back, her breasts teasing his chest.

"A lot." His hands squeezed her ass.

Damn she was getting turned on again. "It shows." She kissed his chest.

"You can come and work out with me, if you'd like."

Her hand paused. He was calling her fat. He wasn't using those words but that was what he meant.

"It was only an offer." He pulled her into him and tipped her chin. "I love your body as it is." He lifted her into his rising erection. "You're so lush and soft." He bent taking a nipple in his mouth.

She dropped the washcloth, her hands clasping at his shoulders and her leg riding up to his waist.

He teased her nipple with his teeth before stepping away from her. She reached for him and he smirked. God, she had no pride where he was concerned.

"I'd love to fuck you right here, but I don't have a condom."

"Oh." How could she forget about that? She didn't want any more kids.

He turned off the water and stepped out, wrapping a towel around his waist. He held out his hand. "Come."

She put hers in his and let him help her out of the shower. He wrapped her in a big towel, pulling her against his body and carrying her into the bedroom. He put her down next to the bed. "Time to dry you off."

By the gleam in his eyes and the bulge under his towel she was pretty sure he was about to make her wetter in some places, but she stood still as he pulled the towel away, running it across her body and then her head, wringing out the water dripping from her hair.

"All dry." He stood. "Now, get on your hands and knees on the bed."

Her legs quivered as she obeyed. She liked this position—a lot. It'd made David seem so much bigger. She couldn't imagine how huge Terry was going to feel like this.

He spread her legs, his touch rough. "This is your punishment for taking out the Ben Wa balls."

"But…" She looked at him over her shoulder. He held his dick in his hand. He already wore a condom. Wetness pooled between her thighs. He was so hard and hot for her. Her. A chubby mother of three was making this exquisite man horny over and over again.

"Unfortunately, I don't think you're ready to take my cock in your ass." His finger trailed down her crease, playing with her butthole.

"No. We can't." She'd never done that. She didn't want to do that. Did she?

He kissed her butt cheek. "We can and we will." He nipped her flesh. "But not tonight. I have to get you ready for that."

"I don't think I'll ever be ready for that."

"You will." He climbed on the bed. "And I think you'll like it." He shoved her legs farther apart. "I know that I'll love it." He rubbed his cock between her thighs. It was thick and hot and hard and she couldn't stop herself from shifting backward. "Oh, you're going to get this all right." He leaned over her, his hands next to hers on the bed. "It's going to be hard and fast." He rubbed against her, his lips tickling her ear. "You're going to pay for disobeying me."

"I'm sorry, Sir." She wiggled against him.

"That's not good enough." He straightened and shoved inside her.

She cried out at the fast intrusion but it was more in surprise than pain. There was a twinge of discomfort as he went deeper than before but mostly it felt wonderful. He pulled almost all the way out and she clamped around him, not wanting to let him leave.

"Fuck, you feel so good." He shoved back in but this time harder and faster.

She dropped her head as her breasts swayed and her body shifted forward and back with his thrusts.

"Don't disobey me again."

"I won't, Sir."

"Never." His thrusts become quicker and more erratic. He was close. She rocked against him. She couldn't be left behind.

"Swear."

"I swear, Sir. Never."

"Not good enough." He swatted her ass as he shoved into her, jarring her more firmly on his cock.

She cried out. That slap, at that exact moment, had made his dick plunge deeper and harder. He was hitting places that had never felt a cock and it was wonderful. She rocked against him and he slapped her again. It was too much and not enough. The sting. The friction. The thrusts. All worked together, making her body tense. His fingers dug into her hips, holding her in place for his invasion. He slapped her again and again, making her muscles contract and squeezing his dick, clinging to him. The pressure, the pleasure was too much. She shattered, her body arching in release and clasping onto him, not letting him leave.

"Fuck, Maggie." He stiffened and followed her into orgasm.

CHAPTER 21: Terry

Terry was stretched out on his back in bed, Maggie draped over him. His hand caressed up and down her spine, loving the feel of her skin, warm, soft and supple. This was not ending tonight. He wouldn't allow it.

"Hmm." She kissed his chest.

"We need to talk."

She stiffened.

"Damn. I didn't mean to say it like that." He was a lawyer. He knew what to say and what not to, but she tangled him all up.

"How did you mean to say it?" She tried to sit but he grabbed her and rolled her onto her back, throwing one leg over her to keep her in place.

"I meant that although I said you could decide what this was, I changed my mind."

"What do you mean by that?" She was looking at him suspiciously.

"I mean, this isn't a two-night fling. I want more."

"Oh." She smiled. "Me too."

"Good." That was easier than he'd thought. He kissed her, a soft brushing of his lips against hers. "But we need to set some rules."

"You and your rules." She rolled her eyes.

"It's better that we both understand exactly what this is."

"What do you mean by that?" she repeated.

There was that tone again. "I mean, you're mine. You don't get to be with anyone else."

"Okay. Same for you."

"Agreed." He kissed her again. Now, came the tough part. "I usually expect my women to be available except when working but I understand about the kids. They come first."

Her eyes hardened a bit and he wanted to slap himself on the forehead. He knew better than to mention other women.

"You're right. They do." She pushed at his chest.

"Good. That's settled." He'd charge right over the goof. He lowered his head to kiss her but she turned away.

"Get off me." She shoved at his chest again.

"Damnit, Maggie." He rolled to his back, letting her sit up. "What do you want me to say? That you're the first woman I've been with? You know better than that."

"You're right. I know exactly what kind of man you are." She scooted off the bed, grabbing a blanket. "I met you at a sex club."

"You were there too." He was sick of this shit.

"By accident."

"Please." He sat up. "You went out, all dressed up to find someone."

"I did not."

He ignored her. "You may not have known what kind of club it was, but you knew you were going to a club."

"I have a right to go out once in a while."

"You're recently divorced and horny. You wanted a man."

"I did not."

"Liar." His eyes held hers. He was a lawyer, a damn good one. "Tell me honestly, that you didn't hope somewhere in that hurt heart of yours that you'd meet someone. Someone nice." He almost spat the word. He was as far from nice as a man could get. "And maybe not that night, but eventually, the two of you would hook up. Have sex. Make love, if calling it that makes you feel better about yourself." This time he rolled his eyes.

She stood there, her mouth opening and closing and her face hot with anger.

"Answer me." He wasn't letting her back away from the truth, not this time.

"Fine. Yes, I guess a part of me hoped that." She looked up at the ceiling, tears in her eyes. "There's nothing wrong with that."

Now, he felt like a heel. He'd wanted to win but he hadn't wanted to make her cry. He lowered his voice. "No, there's nothing at all wrong with that." He took a deep breath. "But don't judge me because I'm more honest about what I want."

"More honest?" Her gaze snapped to his.

"Yes. I want sex and an arrangement. You want the same thing but package it up in your mind as a relationship."

"I don't."

"You don't want sex?" He knew the answer to that.

"Of course, I do. I'm not dead."

He smiled. "No, you're definitely not that."

"But I don't just want to do it."

He laughed. She was still so adorable. "Neither do I."

"You don't?"

"No. I want to go out with you. Take you to lunch. Dinner. Spend time with you. Take care of you." That was going to be a sticking point.

"You do? Really?"

"Yes." He patted the bed. "Now, get back in here so we can finish our discussion."

"Right." The softness in her face fled. "You were going to tell me the exceptions you're making for me that you didn't have to make with all your other women."

He sighed. Damn, he'd hoped she'd forgotten about that. "Yes, I've been in arrangements before."

"No kidding."

"You've been married."

"So, have you."

He tipped his head, conceding that point. "And I don't want to do it again. Is that okay with you?"

She bit her lip. "Yes."

"Truly? Don't think I'll change my mind." At the hurt in her eyes he continued, "It's not that I'm saying this will be temporary. Hell, I don't know how long it'll last and you don't either."

"No. I don't."

"I'm sure you're not ready to jump back into a marriage."

"God, no." She shook her head.

"Then let go of your little girl fantasies. The ones your parents and society drilled into your head from the moment you were born. Discover what *you* want as a woman. They tell you that all girls, all women want...no need a husband and family to be complete. That's great for some but most...well, it doesn't work."

"What should we want? Being alone? Having sex with any man who meets our fancy?"

"You should want what you want. Each woman is different and what each one wants changes with every stage of her life, just like men." He shifted, moving closer to her. "I want you, Maggie and I want more than sex." He lowered his voice. "Although, that is a big part of it."

"No reason to whisper. That's not exactly a secret." She frowned but her eyes sparkled.

"But I also want to help you. Take care of you. And yes, I've done this with a few other women but that was then and this is now. And now, I want you."

"And later?"

He shrugged. "Who knows? You may not want me."

She tipped her head. "That's true. I might tire of your bossy ways."

"You could." He raised the blanket.

"So, how does this work?" She crawled in and he pulled her to his side. "We can see each other when David takes the kids."

"I'd like that." His hand found her skin again, like a compass finding north. He needed to touch this woman. "But I'd like to see you more often than every other weekend."

"I..." She leaned up and kissed him. "Don't take this the wrong way, but I don't want to introduce you to my children."

He kept his face impassive. He should be jumping for joy. He'd been going to suggest that exact thing, but it was different coming from her. He'd loved being around his kids and had been an excellent father. "Just because I belong to a sex club and like to dominate doesn't mean I'm a pedophile." The hurt just slipped out.

"I know that." She touched his cheek. "It's just so soon since the divorce and they already have Stephanie to deal with—"

"Stephanie?"

"David's new wife."

"He's remarried already?"

"Yeah." She smiled sadly. "Six months after the divorce."

"They were seeing each other before."

"No." She shook her head as if to convince herself. "He did not cheat on me."

He raised a brow. "I was a divorce lawyer for a long time. I'd bet he did."

She took a deep breath. "It doesn't matter." She leaned forward and kissed him.

Her lips were soft and sweet and he ran his tongue along her seam until she opened. He slipped inside and it was a warm kiss that promised passion, but not right now. He pulled away.

She sighed. "What were we talking about?"

He was going to kiss her whenever he slipped up. "About your cheating ex and why it doesn't matter, but it does."

"It does?"

"Yes. I'm clean. I have to be in order to be a member of the club, but—"

"*You're* worried about STDs?"

"Yes." He gave her a dirty look. Her tone was more than insulting. "I have to be tested regularly to be an active member of the Club."

"I don't have any sexually transmitted diseases." She sounded appalled that he'd even consider it.

"I'm sure you don't, but I want you to get on birth control and get tested."

"I haven't been with anyone but you since David."

"But we don't know how many women he was with while he was with you."

"Oh...my God. I was tested when I was pregnant with little Davy."

"Afterwards, you and your husband didn't—"

"No." She shook her head. "At first we couldn't and then he left."

"He's a fool but I'm glad." He kissed her again. "Because now, you're mine." He caressed her cheek. "But I still want you to get tested and you need to get on birth control."

"I do need to do that."

"I'm going to pay for all this."

"No. I can—"

"Part of our arrangement is that I take care of you." He put his finger against her lips to stop her from arguing. "I need this. Just like I need to be in control in the bedroom, I need to take care of you."

"I can take care of myself."

"I'm sure you can." He wasn't, not at all. He'd never met a woman who needed to be looked out for more than her. "But I want to do it." Here was the test of her nature. "It'll make me happy."

"Really?"

"Yes." That wasn't a lie.

"Okay. You can pay for the test and the birth control."

"Good girl." He kissed her forehead. Now, for the next hurdle. "I'm going to want to fuck you without a condom. I'll give you the report proving I'm clean."

"You promise you'll only be with me?"

"Yes."

"Okay. I like it better that way anyway."

He stared at her for a long moment. He hadn't expected that battle to be won so easily. He had all his arguments lined up in his head and ready to go.

"What else?"

"Ah...I'm going to want to see you more than every other weekend."

She frowned. "That'll be hard with work and the kids."

"They go to school. We can meet at lunch when you don't have to work."

"Davy's at home."

"He's not in daycare?"

"No."

"Why not?"

"I can't afford it anymore." This time she put her fingers on his lips. "And you're not paying for that."

He kissed her palm and then grabbed her wrist, moving her hand away from his face. "Why not? It'd be for me. The only reason he needs to go is because I want to see you."

"Yes, but I have to take care of myself."

"Why?" He kissed her wrist. "I like taking care of you." He sucked on her thumb before nipping it. "Both in and out of the bedroom."

She pulled her hand away. "I can't. I just can't." She sat up, scooting away from him. "I'm in this mess because I relied on

David for everything. I can't do that anymore."

"It's not your fault you picked an asshole."

"Then whose fault is it?" She climbed out of bed again, tucking the blanket around her. "No one made me marry him. No one made me quit my job. Quit college." She tapped her chest. "I did that. I wanted marriage and kids and now look at me."

He crawled out of bed and pulled her into his arms. She buried her face in his chest, her shoulders shaking from her sobs.

"I'm a mess. I can't afford my home. I can't afford day care. I can barely afford the babysitter. My car is a wreck and...and I work at Outback and barely make enough to pay the bills."

"Shhh." He picked her up.

"Stop."

"Hush." He put her in the bed and she rolled away from him. He dropped down beside her pulling her close. "It's okay." He kissed the back of her head. "Let me take care of everything. I'm good at it. I like doing it." He kissed her again. "Please."

"I want to but I can't. It's not right."

"It's not wrong." He was starting to lose patience. "You need help. Let me help you."

"I won't take your money."

He held his breath and counted to ten. Yelling at her would only make her cry harder and he hated her tears. "Okay. That's fine. Let's start with something simple."

She rolled over, looking up at him. "What on that list is simple?"

"The car."

"I'm not taking your car either."

"Okay, but you can borrow it."

"It's your daughter's present."

"She didn't want it. She wanted a European tour."

"Then why did you keep it."

This would be a good time to lie, but he wouldn't. "I was going to give it to her when she returned, but she doesn't know that. Now, I'd rather loan"—he stressed the word—"it to you."

"I have to put my kids in there. They'll mess it all up."

"I don't care. It's worth it to know that you're safe."

"No, really. Three kids in that car. They'll destroy it."

"You're right." He kissed her nose. This should seal the deal. "You need a minivan."

"What?" Her body stiffened.

"We'll go to the dealer early tomorrow and we'll get you one." He skimmed his hand down her back, loving the way she instinctively relaxed into his touch.

"No. Absolutely not." She slapped his chest.

So much for relaxing. "You need a car. I'm not going to worry all day and night that you got mugged by some Uber driver or that another piece of shit car you drive is broken down somewhere."

"You'd really worry?"

The way she was looking at him made his heart stutter. "Yes, I'd really worry." He stroked his thumb over the soft skin of her cheek. "I care about you."

"You barely know me."

"So. I know you're kind and giving." He grinned. "Sexy and yet innocent."

"I have three kids. I'm hardly innocent."

"There's a difference between being a virgin and being

innocent."

"I suppose."

"The car or the minivan?"

"Car. But it's only until I can get something else, or I can make payments to you."

"We can talk about that later." Like never.

"Thank you." She kissed him softly.

"Let's get some sleep. Tomorrow we can talk about how we can meet around your kids' schedules and work."

"Okay."

He stretched out and she snuggled against his side, her hand on his chest and her leg tangled with his. He loved the feeling of her soft skin against his. "You wouldn't consider quitting your job, would you?"

"No. I need the money."

"Hmm." He wasn't going to offer to pay her again. He'd learned that lesson.

CHAPTER 22: Maggie

Maggie hurried into her house, overloaded with groceries. She should've asked Terry how many of his friends were coming to help, but it hadn't been top on her mind last night. This morning, she hadn't had the heart to wake him. He'd looked so sweet sleeping—his usually stern face relaxed, his broad back bare, the blanket tossed carelessly over his hips. It'd taken every ounce of will power she'd had not to run her hands down all that smooth skin and then follow the same path with her lips. God, that man turned her on. Unfortunately, she'd been a good girl and had gone to the grocery store.

If these guys were coming to help, even if it were only two additional men, she'd need to feed them lunch. She dropped the bags on the table and began putting away the groceries. She'd bought more than she could afford, but this was still a lot cheaper than hiring movers. She could forego sleep and pack everything herself but the moving…She would've had to hire someone to help with that.

The doorbell rang as she stuffed the last six pack of beer in the fridge. She hurried to the door and opened it. "Terry…"

A short, curvy brunette and a tall, handsome man with brown hair and a friendly smile stared at her. He was carrying a catering dish, as well as bags of groceries strapped over his arm. The young woman also held bags of food.

"May I help you?"

"I'm Annie and this is Patrick." The young woman pointed at the guy.

Maggie's gaze went over their heads as another car stopped, parking on the curb and a man and woman got out.

Annie glanced at them when the car door closed. "Hey, Sarah. Hey, Nick."

"Hey," said the man who had dark hair and looked kind of familiar. "I told you Annie would bring food."

"You're lucky she likes to feed you guys." The woman was tall and slender with red hair. "Hey, Annie. Patrick."

"I am lucky." Nick's arm went around her, his hand resting on her lower back as they stopped behind the other couple.

Annie turned back toward Maggie, the smile slipping from her face. "Oh, my God. Terry did tell you that he invited us over to help, didn't he?" She turned and looked at Patrick. "He wouldn't not tell her, would he?"

"Terry probably just ordered it to be done and expected it to happen," said Nick.

Maggie didn't like Nick's comment about Terry, even if it were kind of true. "Of course, he told me. I-I was just surprised." She'd expected Terry to be here when his friends arrived. She stepped aside. "Please, come inside and thank you for doing this."

The four bustled through the doorway.

"You're welcome and where's the kitchen?" asked Annie.

"This way." Maggie led them into the other room. "You didn't have to bring anything. I have more than enough for lunch."

"Lunch?" Annie laughed. "You assumed these goons ate breakfast.

"Ah…" She had assumed that.

"I'm starving." Nick was already pawing through the bags of groceries, pulling out bagels, cream cheese, fruit and other items.

Patrick put the catering dish down and set up the warming pan. "Eggs, bacon, sausage and anything else you can think of." He pulled off the lid.

"Oh my, that smells wonderful." Maggie's mouth watered. She was starving.

"Thanks." Annie beamed as she put juices and plastic cups on the table. "I love to cook and these guys love to eat. It's a win-win."

"Thank you. I hadn't thought about breakfast." She was going to kill Terry. He could've told her what to expect.

"No problem." Annie handed her a plate. "Sarah and I figured that Terry wouldn't give you all the info you needed." She shook her head. "These men are like cavemen. They don't understand how things work."

"Hey," said Patrick around a mouthful of food. "We know how things work."

"We just don't care." Nick stuffed more bacon in his mouth. "That's what we have you two for."

"Among other things." Patrick sent Annie a look that threatened to scorch the paint off the walls.

"Oh…" Maggie flushed and grabbed a bagel.

"It takes a while, but you get used to them." Sarah handed Maggie an orange juice. "They're all great guys, but they are guys through and through."

"You love that about us," said Nick.

"That I do." Sarah's gaze warmed as she looked at him.

Maggie's heart almost wept. That was love in those eyes, both sets. She was happy for them and so damn jealous. It'd been so long since David had looked at her like that.

"So, who else is coming?" asked Annie as she ate some eggs off Patrick's plate.

"I'm not sure."

"So, he didn't tell you." Nick snorted. "No surprise there."

"He told me he invited his friends and I didn't ask for details." There was no reason for Nick to talk about Terry in that tone.

"She's perfect for him," muttered Patrick.

"Ah…" She wasn't sure what to say about that. "I would've asked but I was at work and…"

"And then you were busy." Sarah nudged Nick. "We understand perfectly."

Maggie blushed. "No, it's not…" It was exactly like the other woman thought.

"Where is he anyway?" Nick looked around.

"Uhm, at home."

"Home? What's he doing there?" asked Nick. "Probably, still sleeping."

"Yes, but I left early to go to the store and didn't want to wake him."

"Why the hell not?" Nick pulled out his phone. "I'll wake

his lazy ass."

"He's not lazy." She didn't like this Nick guy.

Nick stepped into the living room and Sarah smiled softly at her. "It's the way the two of them are. It's weird at first, but you get used to it."

"Yeah," said Patrick. "They're always bickering but both of them would do whatever they could for the other."

"Kind of like siblings," said Annie. "I have five brothers and these two act just like them." She pointed toward the living room. "Speaking of brothers. Hey, Mattie."

Nick was at the door, waving in the mechanic from the garage and three other people, two guys and a petite redhead.

"Hey, Maggie. Good to see you again." Mattie smiled at her as he walked into the kitchen and went straight to the food. "Leena, Annie brought those bagels you love."

The little redhead hurried into the kitchen, pushing past all the large men and grabbing two bagels. "Thank you, Annie. You're a lifesaver. I was starving." She stuffed a hunk in her mouth.

"Hi," Maggie said to the girl. She looked different not covered in grease, but it was the same young woman who'd talked to her in the garage.

"Hey," said Leena.

"Where do you want us to start?" asked Annie.

"Uhm..."

The doorbell rang. Good lord, how many people had Terry invited. Nick opened the door, stuffing his phone in his pocket. Ethan walked in looking exhausted.

"Didn't expect to see you after working all night," said Nick.

"Like you got a lot of sleep." Ethan pushed past Nick and

went straight to the kitchen. He gave Sarah and Annie a quick kiss on their cheeks before turning to Maggie. "So, where's Terry?"

"On his way," said Nick. "I just woke his ass up."

Ethan smiled. "I'm sure he was up late." His blue eyes darted to Maggie and she blushed.

"I'll get you guys started in my daughter's room." Isabella had wanted to pack her own stuff but she'd have to get over it. Maggie was going to get as much done as possible while she had help. "The other bedrooms are almost done."

"We can load the van," said Leena.

"We'll start with the furniture," said Mattie, shoveling his breakfast into his mouth.

"Sounds perfect." She smiled at them. It must be wonderful to have so many friends. Terry was a lucky man. Besides her kids, she had no one.

CHAPTER 23: Terry

Terry got out of the car and had to force himself not to slam the door. Maggie's place looked like she was having a huge party. He was glad his friends had all come through for him, but she should've woken him.

"Hey, Terry. Almost ready with the first load. Just filling in the gaps with some boxes." Mattie jumped down from the U-Haul truck. "Where are we going?"

"I'll let you know in a minute. Where's Maggie?"

"Last time I saw her she was in one of the boys' rooms."

"Great." He headed toward the house. "Thanks for coming to help."

"Sure thing." Mattie tagged along after him. "You okay?"

"Yeah. Why?" He walked inside, nodding at Patrick who was on his way out with a large box.

"You look...kind of pissed."

"I'm fine." He glanced at Mattie. "But Maggie and I need to talk. Alone."

"Right." Mattie spun around. "I'll grab a box and go

outside."

Terry strode down the hallway, glancing inside first one room and then the next. There she was. He walked into the older boy's room.

She glanced up and smiled at him as she closed a box. "Hi."

"Where the hell did you sneak off to this morning?" He'd been furious when he'd woken, hard and ready for a fuck, and found himself alone.

"I had to get groceries." She straightened, the smile disappearing from her face.

"Why? I had food at the house."

"Not for me. For your friends."

"Why are you feeding my friends?" Women made no sense.

"It's the least I can do since they're helping me move."

He stepped closer to her. "You know, I arranged it, right?"

"Yes and thank you again." She looked puzzled but she'd figure it out soon.

He stopped in front of her, close enough to smell her—vanilla and woman, an aphrodisiac. "Then, the least you could've done is stayed with me." He kissed her, loving how she opened for him without any hesitation, her body leaning into his. "I missed you this morning." He took her hand and placed it on his rising cock.

"I'll make it up to you later, Sir." She gave him a slight squeeze and he moaned against her lips.

"Damn right, you will." He swatted her ass as she stepped away.

"I think, I'm done in here."

"Great. I'll tell the guys this room is ready to load up." He bent and grabbed the box. "Oh, where are they going? Mattie said the truck is almost full."

"Already? That was fast."

"Lots of muscle." He flexed his arms and loved the spark of heat that lighted her eyes.

"Tell him, Southshore Apartments. Apartment two—"

"Southshore? That place is a dump."

"It's not that bad."

"Not that bad? Compared to what? A Turkish prison?"

"Well, that's where we're moving." Her voice cracked a little.

Terry winced. She was going to cry. He dropped the box and pulled her to him. "No, baby. We can figure out something else."

"No, *we* can't." She pushed away from him. "I can't afford anything else and I'm not taking your money."

"You won't be taking it. I'll pay your rent—"

"That's the same as taking your money and I won't do it."

"You agreed to let me take care of you."

"Not with money." She moved past him but he grabbed her arm.

"You are not moving there." This was not up for discussion.

"You can't stop me."

"Watch me." He stormed out of the bedroom. "Everyone. We're done. Unload everything back into the house."

"Terry, stop." Maggie trailed after him, clutching at his shirt, but he ignored her.

"What's going on?" Patrick glanced from Terry to Maggie and then to Annie who'd just stepped out of the little girl's bedroom with Sarah.

"Change of plans. Maggie's not moving. Not yet anyway."

"Okaaay." Nick dropped the box he was carrying and headed for the door. "I'll tell Mattie and the guys."

"Wait." Maggie grabbed Terry's hand and he let her pull him into the baby's room. "I already signed the lease."

"I'll get you out of it."

"You can't."

"I can. I'm a lawyer." This was easy to fix.

"But I have to move. This is the only place I can afford. I looked at other places. Trust me. Southshore was not my first choice."

"Don't worry. We'll find something else. Something nicer. Closer to my place." He pulled her flush against him. "I can sneak over when the kids go to sleep—"

"Stop." She stepped away from him. "Just stop. Okay. This is it. This is where I have to live."

"Stop being so fucking stubborn."

"I will when you stop being so thickheaded."

"I'm not the one being thickheaded. I understand how this works. I take care of you and making sure you don't live in a neighborhood where you could get shot in a drive-by is part of taking care of you."

"For how long? I can't move to one house and in a few months to another. Isabella and Peter are in school and moving is hard on them."

"You can stay here."

"I can't." Her voice was shrill. "Listen to me. I can't afford this and part of you taking care of me is not me taking your money."

"Yes, it is." This was getting old. He'd never had a woman

fight him so much. Of course, his other women had all been well off but they never cared when he bought them things.

She took a deep breath. "Let me help you see this from my point of view."

"Okay." It wasn't going to change anything but he'd listen and later, he'd use her words against her like any good attorney.

"Let's say, I take your offer and you move me and the kids to a place near your house."

"Sounds good so far."

Her lips thinned. "And then in three months or six months, this ends."

"It might not." He couldn't imagine getting tired of her that soon, but it was possible.

"No, it might not, but it might. If it does, I'm going to have to move again and that's hard on the kids and me." She touched his cheek. "I appreciate your offer. I really do"—she leaned up and kissed him—"but I need to move to a place I can afford on my own."

His hands went to her hips and he rested his chin on the top of her head. She wasn't going to like this. "No."

"What?" She tried to back away but he tightened his grip, keeping her near. "You can't just tell me no."

"I can. I did." Damnit, that wasn't the right answer. "Think of your kids. You don't want them living in that area."

"No, I don't but I have no choice."

"You do and before you get all ruffled listen to me." He cupped her cheek. "I'd never leave you hanging with no money and no place to live. Even after it was over."

"You say that now—"

"I mean it."

"So did David and look at what that got me." She tore his hand from her hip and stepped away from him.

"I am not your fucking ex-husband." He was yelling now, but that comparison was too low to let pass. "I would never leave my wife, ex-wife, in such a financial mess that she'd have to move herself and kids...my kids...to a slum."

"You're lucky. You have the money to make those promises."

"Your ex can't be that fucking broke."

"I told you, business was bad for years before our divorce."

"I will not leave you with no place to go." He was sick of her defending the bastard. She trusted that asshole more than she trusted him. "If you don't believe me, I can put money in your account or we can sign a contract. Whatever you want."

"What I want is to not be treated like your whore," she yelled. "Why can't you understand that?"

That was it. This woman pushed all his buttons. "The only difference between what I'm suggesting and what you did with your fuckhead ex-husband is a piece of fucking paper."

"We were married."

"You fucked him for a roof over your head." As soon as he said the words, he regretted them. "Maggie..."

Her face was pale and her eyes wide, but her voice was soft. "Get out."

"Maggie..." He stepped toward her and she backed away so fast she tripped over a box and landed on her ass on her son's bed.

"Get out. Now." She scrambled up and hurried past him.

He followed but she ducked into the bathroom.

"Maggie. Please." He rested his head against the door.

"Go away." She was crying now and he felt like a piece of shit.

A large hand landed on his shoulder. "Terry, come on," said Nick.

"Fuck you." He shoved Nick away and hit the door. "Maggie, come out here right now. Let me explain."

"Go away."

"Terry." Sarah's voice was smooth and calm. "You guys should go. Annie and I will stay." Her hand on his arm was soft and fleeting. "You can come back later and talk to her, but right now, you should go."

"Fuck." He hit his head against the door. "Maggie, talk to me."

The only sound he heard was her crying.

CHAPTER 24: Terry

Terry turned and shoved past Nick and the others. Everyone stared at him like he had two heads. "Fuck off. All of you." He stormed out of the house and toward his car.

Ethan ran up to him and grabbed his arm. "Come on. I'll drive."

"I don't need you to fucking drive." He jerked free from his friend.

"Think, Terry." Ethan stepped in front of him. "Leaving your car here is an excellent reason to come back later." He glanced at the house. "After she's settled down."

Terry ran his hand through his hair. He should've thought of that. "Let's go." He headed toward Ethan's car.

"Club?" asked Nick.

"Yeah. See you there." Ethan got into his car and drove down the street. He glanced at Terry. "What the fuck?"

"I don't want to talk about it."

"Yeah, but—"

"Don't. Okay." He turned toward Ethan. "I don't need to

hear shit from you and then from the rest of the assholes. Once will be more than enough." He knew his friends. Hell, if one of them had done what he did, he'd be the first to give them a hard time.

"Fair enough," said Ethan.

By the time Nick, Patrick and Mattie arrived at the Club, Terry was on his second drink.

"Damn," said Nick as he and the others walked into Ethan's office. "A little early to be drinking."

"Like you can talk. I remember you being drunk all day and night not too long ago." Here it came. All the shit he didn't want to hear.

Nick grabbed a beer instead of his usual scotch. "Yeah, but that was when I was..." He pursed his lips as if in thought. "What did you call me after Sarah left me hanging?" He smiled and it was like a kick in the balls. "Right, pussy-whipped. That was when I was pussy-whipped." He raised his brow, a smirk on his face. "Is that what's wrong with you?"

Patrick laughed. "Oh, how far you've fallen. The man who'll never marry again."

"I won't." He'd never repeat that nightmare.

"Now, that everyone is here." Ethan tipped his chair, balancing on the two back legs. "What the fuck were you thinking?"

"I...Shit." Obviously, he hadn't been thinking. He tossed back his drink.

"You know better than that," said Ethan.

"Everyone knows better than to call the woman he wants a whore," said Mattie, who was sitting at the bar sipping a soda.

"Unless she likes that," said Nick. "But I don't think Maggie's that kind of lady."

"She's not." Terry refilled his glass from the bottle that was next to it on the table.

"Seriously, what got into you?" asked Ethan. "You can be a big-mouthed ass, but I've never seen you like this."

"She's driving me crazy." He rested the glass against his forehead.

"You two have fucked, right?" asked Nick .

"Yes. Numerous times." He gave Nick the death glare. "I'm not you. I have no intentions of being celibate for anyone."

"We'll see." Nick's smug look was making Terry want to punch him in the face. "Ethan get the book. I want to place a bet on Terry and Maggie."

"I'm in." Patrick leaned against the bar drinking a beer. "I got fifty on Terry and Maggie living together within three months."

Ethan pulled out the book and started writing.

"Not going to happen," said Terry.

"I got your back, buddy." Mattie smiled at him. "Put me down for six months."

"Fuck off." Terry was sick of his friends but he didn't have a car. Plus, he didn't feel like going home and drinking alone.

"Put me down for under two months," said Nick. "And I want to bet that Terry does something even stupider than what he did today." He smirked. "Terry is going to fuck this thing up big time. I can feel it." He took a swallow of his beer. "My intuition is always right."

"Yeah. You're a fucking fortune teller." Terry snorted.

"I was right about Sarah and about Patrick and Annie."

"He has you there," said Patrick. "You should listen to Nick. He helped me stop being so thickheaded about Annie."

Two times today he'd been called stupid. It was two times too many. "No, Nick should listen to me before he ends up broke and alone."

"Don't fucking start," said Nick. "This is about you being a dick. This has nothing to do with me and Sarah."

"You brought up your intuition and I'm telling you that it sucks. No. Actually, your intuition is probably good, but you're not listening to it. You're listening to your dick."

"Fuck off." Nick's eyes were like coal.

"I should. I should leave you alone and let you learn this lesson the hard way, but fuck me, I can't. Jesus, Nick, think for once. We talked about this years ago and we all agreed that prenups were a necessity. Come to my office and let's get one written up." He liked Nick. They fought and argued but he truly liked the younger man.

"Sarah and I don't need a prenup."

"God." He tipped his head back and laughed. "You are so fucking naïve."

"Just because your wife left, took your house and your kids and supported her lesbian lover with the money from your practice, doesn't mean that's going to happen to me and Sarah." Nick's eyes narrowed. "I know how to satisfy her so she won't be leaving me for anyone, especially a woman."

"Fuck, Nick." Ethan jumped up at the same time Patrick and Mattie moved forward.

Terry shook his head. "You think I'm going to fight this dumbass for that? Not worth it. Plus, except for the part about me not satisfying women, it's true." And it still fucking hurt. "No reason to get mad about the truth." He tossed back his drink. "If Nick were mature, he'd realize that what I said is also true." He refilled his glass.

Nick stared at him for a long moment. "I'm not signing a prenup."

He took a deep breath. "Please, come by my office and we can talk."

"No." Nick walked to the bar and tossed his bottle in the trash before grabbing another beer. "We don't need one."

"It won't hurt to talk to him," said Ethan.

"How did this become about me?" Nick looked at Ethan. "I'm not the one whose girlfriend is crying in her bathroom because she was just called a whore."

"Worse than that, she was told she'd been a whore her entire life," corrected Patrick.

"That's not what I meant."

"That's exactly what you said." Patrick walked away from the bar and took a seat. "What the hell got into you?"

"Did you hear where she thinks she's moving?"

"Southshore," said Mattie. "I'm pretty sure the neighbors five houses down heard you guys shouting about that."

"You know what kind of area that is?" Terry looked around.

"Yeah," said Patrick. "Not a good one."

"Right. You wouldn't let Annie live there, would you?"

"Hell, no," said Patrick.

"Exactly, but Maggie won't listen. She can't afford any place else but she refuses to let me help her."

"So, she's a whore because she won't take your money?" Ethan laughed. "I think you should look up the definition of the word."

"I said taking my money was no different than letting her husband support her."

"Oh yeah, we all heard that." Mattie snickered. "You called every older woman in the world whores, including all grandmas."

"Well, they are."

"Jesus, Terry." Patrick rolled his eyes. "You're one sick bastard."

"He has a point," said Ethan. "Women have been trading their bodies for hundreds of years."

"Stop with your sales pitch. We've all"—Nick looked at his brother—"except perhaps Mattie, heard you use that line to convince some girl to work for you."

Ethan shrugged. "It works because it's true."

"Didn't work so well for Terry," mumbled Mattie and he and Nick laughed.

Terry shifted on the couch. The alcohol, no breakfast and not much sleep was wearing on him. "Tease me all you want. I don't give a shit. I need to figure out how to fix this."

"Start with an apology," said Patrick. "A big one and then"—he grinned—"eat her pussy until she forgives you."

"I don't need pointers on how to fix the fight. I can handle that."

"You sure?" Nick glanced at Ethan. "She seemed pretty pissed."

"I can get past that, but I'm having issues getting her to let me help her."

"Don't ask," said Mattie. "Just do it."

"I can't force her to move somewhere I choose."

"Why bother with that?" Mattie stood and tossed his soda

can in the trash. "Her house is for sale, right?"

"Yeah. So?"

"Buy it." Mattie shrugged. "Then she doesn't have to move at all."

He stared at the kid. "That's a fucking brilliant idea."

"Not gonna work," said Nick. "If she won't take your money, there's no way she'll let you buy her a house."

"I'm not going to tell her."

"Your name is going to be all over those documents," said Nick.

"Please. I'm a lawyer. There are ways to get around that."

"She's going to find out," warned Patrick.

"Only if one of you fuckers opens your big mouth. So, don't."

"I won't say anything, but I still don't think this is a good idea," said Patrick.

CHAPTER 25: Maggie

Maggie sat in the bathroom, too embarrassed to come out. Terry had called her a whore in front of all his friends. They were probably laughing at her or whispering about her right now. She was such an idiot. Men like Terry didn't fall for women like her; they used them.

There was a tap on the door.

"Everyone's gone except me and Annie. Why don't you come out and we can talk?" It was Sarah's soft voice.

Maggie took a long, shaky breath, trying to compose herself. "Thanks for staying but you should go with your boyfriends." She didn't want to see anyone right now, especially someone who'd heard their fight.

"Too late." It was Annie's louder tone. "They aren't coming back for a while. You're stuck with us."

"If you aren't ready to come out, that's fine," said Sarah. "We understand, but it's better to talk about it. Trust me on that one."

"There's nothing to talk about."

"Okay." Sarah's tone was hesitant. "Would you like us to finish packing your daughter's room?"

"No." She moved to the sink and splashed water on her face. These two weren't going to leave, so she might as well face them. She opened the door and smiled but it was tremulous. "I can finish it later. You should call..." She couldn't remember their boyfriends' names. "I appreciate you staying, but you don't need to babysit me."

"We're not doing that. Not at all." Annie took her hand. "Come on. Let's have some dessert." She tugged and Maggie let the younger woman drag her down the hallway.

"Food is Annie's answer to everything," muttered Sarah as she followed them. "I'm going to be five hundred pounds if I keep hanging out with her."

Maggie and Annie both threw Sarah a disgusted look.

"You're always going to be thin," said Annie. "Me on the other hand." She slapped her own ass. "I've got to watch it already."

"I'd kill to be your size again." Maggie looked at the other woman who was curvy but still with the tightness of someone much younger than herself.

"You look great." Annie pushed her toward a chair and went to the fridge, pulling out a bag from the back. "I had to hide these or the guys would've gobbled them up with breakfast." She opened the bag and pulled out a container of bakery cookies.

Sarah took one and bit into it. "Not as good as the ones you made, Maggie, but still yummy."

"You tried my cookies?"

"Yeah. We made Terry share." Sarah grinned. "I think Nick

and Ethan ate more than he did."

"I'd love to try them," said Annie.

"The kids finished the ones I'd left here, but I do have some cupcakes." She stood and walked to the metal cake box on the counter. "Isabella needed them for a school party. I always make extra in case some don't turn out." She carried it to the table and removed the lid. "These are a little messed up. I sent the best ones to school."

"They're beautiful." Annie's eyes drifted over the display.

"Thanks. These are yellow cake with milk chocolate frosting." Maggie pointed at one set. "And these are strawberry with butter cream frosting." There were assorted sprinkles garnishing the tops.

"They look delicious." Sarah grabbed one with chocolate frosting and dark sprinkles. She tore off the paper and took a large bit. "Mmm. Maggie, you are a god in the kitchen."

"Thank you." Maggie blushed as she started the coffee.

"Alcohol," said Sarah. "I think we need something to drink and I don't mean coffee."

"Good idea." Annie moved to the fridge. "Wine and cupcakes. My favorite."

"Sorry. I don't have any wine." She couldn't afford that luxury.

"Don't worry. I came prepared." Annie grabbed a bottle of wine from the fridge.

"You expected this?" She glanced from one woman to the other.

"No." Annie laughed. "But I did think that a glass of wine would be nice when we were done helping you move."

"You were right about that." Maggie turned off the coffee

pot and grabbed three of the disposable cups that Annie had brought, placing them on the table. She could nap before the kids came home.

"You don't happen to have Crown Royale, do you?" asked Sarah.

"No. Sorry. I did buy a few six packs of beer."

"That'll work. Annie, grab me one." Sarah finished her cupcake. "I prefer my sweets to be baked not drank."

"More for us." Annie handed a beer to Sarah and then opened the wine, pouring some in two of the three cups before grabbing one of the strawberry cupcakes. She took a bite. "Oh, my, these are fabulous."

"Thank you. I love to bake." Maggie took a sip. "I'm sorry you had to hear all that and I'm not a—"

"Oh, honey." Annie leaned over and hugged her. "We know that. Terry can be..."

"A real jerk," said Sarah.

"He's brusque." Maggie shook her head. "I'm such a fool. He calls me a whore and I still stick up for him."

"You're not a fool." Annie smiled. "It's what we do when we care for someone."

"I don't. I can't." She took another drink. "I barely know him."

"Yeah," Sarah sighed. "That's their secret power, this group of guys. We fall for them hard and we barely know them." She smiled. "But the good thing is, they're all good guys and all this"—she waved her hand around—"crap is worth it in the end."

"I'm glad for you, but it's not the same with me and Terry."

"Really?" Annie's brown eyes were amused.

"No. I mean, we just met and I'm recently divorced and...uhm, things happened but this wasn't going anywhere anyway and now, it's over."

"Are you sure about that?" asked Sarah.

"Yes. I'm not going to be with a guy who thinks I'm a whore. I mean, how can I?" Part of her wanted them to explain, make some sense of this so she could be with Terry again. The way he made her feel...She wasn't ready to give that up.

"I agree," said Sarah.

"You do?" asked Annie, surprised.

"Yes, but I don't think Terry actually feels that way about you."

"He said it." She finished her wine and refilled her glass, topping off Annie's.

"Terry can be, as you said, brusque," said Sarah.

"Yes, but he told me he's always honest. So, he honestly thinks I'm a whore." She almost cried. She'd thought that the things they'd done had been special but apparently, only to her.

"He actually called all women whores not just you." Sarah picked another cupcake from the dish.

"What?" She hadn't heard him say that.

"He said that we trade our bodies for comfort, companionship, and a roof over our heads all the time."

"He's right. Somewhat." Annie sipped her drink. "Nowadays, most women have jobs but in the past that's kind of how it worked."

"I guess, but I still didn't appreciate it." She let this tumble through her brain, not sure if she agreed or not.

"Terry's an acquired taste," said Sarah. "He doesn't like me, but he's always polite. I get the feeling that he'll do anything and I mean anything for someone he cares about."

"Like Nick." Annie's tone was soft.

Maggie watched the two of them, not sure what they were talking about.

"Sorry," said Sarah. "You need some background. Nick and I are engaged."

"Oh, congratulations." She was glad for the other woman but so empty inside.

"Thanks, but Terry's not happy about it," said Sarah.

"He dislikes you that much?" Maggie couldn't understand what Terry didn't like about the quiet, younger woman.

"Yes and no. He's upset because Nick won't sign a prenup." Sarah put some frosting on her finger and licked it off. "This is delicious."

"Oh. Nick has money."

"They all have money," said Annie. "Membership at La Petite Mort Club is not cheap."

"They're all members. All the men that were here?"

"Not Mattie's friends and not Leena." Annie looked at Sarah. "But we're members."

"It's not just for men?" She'd never considered that women would want to go there. Work there, yes, but go there?

"Heavens no. There are a lot of rich women who want some kink in their lives too." Annie grinned. "Ask Sarah. She joined before she met Nick. I joined after I met Patrick."

"You worked there." Sarah laughed. "And I was a one-time contract. Not a member."

"Oh my." Her eyes had to be as big as dessert plates.

"Yes, oh my." Sarah smiled. "So, trust me, nothing that happened between you and Terry will surprise either of us."

"Oh, no. It wasn't like that." She clamped her mouth shut. *He ate his dessert from my body, but nothing like stuff that went on in a sex club.*

"Sure. Keep telling yourself that." Annie patted her hand. "However, think about what you'll be giving up if you end it with him." Her eyes got dreamy. "All those long nights and days of fabulous sex." She sighed. "Patrick would have to do something really stupid for me to toss him to the curb."

"Calling you a whore isn't enough?" It was for her.

Annie's smile faltered. "No, but it almost was."

"He called you a whore?" Sarah was shocked. "You never told me that."

"He didn't use those exact words but it still hurt."

"And you worked through it?" Maybe, she could too.

"Yeah. He swore he didn't mean it and I believed him." She shrugged. "Stupid? Maybe. But we're happy now and I couldn't find a kinder and more caring guy."

"I don't know." She wasn't sure she should share this, but...She took a big gulp of her wine. "This wasn't the first time."

"He called you a whore before?" Annie's eyes sparked with anger. "I'm going to have a long talk with him."

"What exactly happened?" asked Sarah.

"He offered me money to...you know."

"Just out of the blue?" Sarah looked at Annie. "That doesn't sound like Terry. If he wanted to pay, he could have a woman from the Club."

"Well, no. We were...kissing and I got a call and had to go to work. He wanted me to stay with him but I need the money so he offered to pay me to stay home."

"Oh. He didn't call you a whore." Annie laughed. "That's his way of solving a problem. The man has so much money and has had for quite a while that he believes everything can be solved by throwing money at it."

"Unfortunately, he's right most of the time," said Sarah.

"That must be why he was so pissed at you." Annie's eyes sparkled. "You're the one thing he can't buy and it's driving him crazy."

"I don't know about that. " She had agreed to use his car.

"No, that's it." Annie almost vibrated off her chair. "Terry's a true dominant. He has to be in charge." She grinned. "I'm sure that's no secret to you."

"No." Maggie flushed. "I'm quite aware of his predilections, but only in the bedroom or bedroom activities."

"And he agreed to that?" asked Sarah.

"Yeah. Why?"

Sarah sent Annie a knowing look.

"Oh, this is perfect." Annie's grin widened.

"What am I missing?" She looked from one to the other.

"Oh, Terry has it bad for you." Annie hugged her again. "You poor thing."

"I don't think that's the case." Her heart beat an unsteady rhythm of hope and disbelief.

"It is if he agreed to only be in control in the bedroom," said Sarah. "Terry always likes to be in control. Always."

"He does try outside of the bedroom." She'd never met a bossier man or a sexier one.

"And you usually let him, don't you?" Sarah studied her.

"Yeah. Most of the time, it's fine. I don't mind." She actually liked it.

"Except when it comes to money," said Annie. "Oh, the two of you are in for so much fun."

"If you enjoy fighting," mumbled Sarah around her cupcake. "Not everyone does."

"I don't." Maggie glanced at the other two women. "You two do?"

"Sometimes." Sarah's eyes grew distant. "Not the actual fight but the sex."

"Make-up sex is nice." It'd been good with David. It was sure to be fabulous with Terry. Not that she was making-up with him or anything.

"Oh, not just the make-up sex," said Sarah. "The fighting sex. Nick and I both get so turned on whenever we're fighting that we can't keep our hands to ourselves."

"Really?" She'd never heard of having sex during an argument.

"Yeah, me and Patrick too, but I also love to argue," said Annie. "Patrick is pretty easy going but sometimes when I push that button. Oh, it's really, really nice." She finished her wine and sighed. "Give Terry a chance to explain. Deep down, he's a good guy and he could use someone like you in his life."

"This thing we have isn't like that." It was just sex. That was all.

"That's what Annie and I thought about our situations too."

"No. really. I have three kids and Terry isn't interested in being around them. Honestly, I don't want him around them."

"Terry would never hurt a child." Annie's tone wasn't as friendly.

"I know he wouldn't on purpose, but I can't have him becoming a part of our lives and then disappearing. Kids don't understand that. The divorce was hard enough." She shook her head. "No matter what, I'm not introducing a man into their lives unless I know it's a long-term commitment. That's not what Terry and I have." They just had the hots for each other.

"Oh, this is excellent." Annie grinned. "Keep him at arm's length except in the bedroom. It drives these guys crazy. Doesn't it, Sarah."

Sarah finished her beer. "Yes, it does and I'm talking from experience." She stood and walked to the fridge, grabbing another beer. "You keep this up and you and Terry will be living together soon."

"Right." She laughed but the other women just smiled. "Oh, that's not going to happen. It can't. I won't let it."

The other two looked and each other and burst out laughing.

CHAPTER 26: Maggie

Maggie sat up in bed, her head pounding. She shouldn't have had all that wine. The doorbell rang. She was pretty sure that was what had woken her. She hoped it was Terry because she was in the perfect mood to give him a piece of her mind.

She opened the door and the words "What do you want?" froze on her tongue.

"Hey mom," her daughter walked past her and stopped.

"You packed?" Isabella glared at her. "You didn't pack my room, did you?"

"Honey, I'm sorry but—"

"You promised I could do it." Isabella stormed down the hallway toward her bedroom.

"Did you get the message?" David handed Davy to her.

"What message?" She scanned the yard. Terry's car was gone. He must've come by while she was sleeping. He hadn't even tried to apologize. She should be glad, but instead she wanted to cry.

"Can I build a fort?" Peter started moving boxes without

waiting for her answer.

"Kathy tried calling you." David was almost bouncing with excitement.

"Kathy? Kathy who?" She bent, putting Davy down by his brother.

"Our agent. She said she tried calling you."

"She did?" She hadn't looked at her phone for hours. Her stomach churned. If Kathy called and David was excited, it could only mean one thing. "Someone made an offer." She prayed it was low but by the way David was acting, she didn't think this prayer would be any more successful than the last several hundred.

"Yes. Full price. Can you believe it?"

"Oh, that's great." It was, kind of.

"The buyer wants to move so..." David handed her a manila folder. "Here's the paperwork. You need to sign it."

"I'll look it over."

"Just sign It, Margaret."

He always called her Margaret when he was angry with her. "I'm not signing anything without looking it over."

"Fine, but hurry up. This guy wants to buy now. We need to accept his offer before he looks at something else."

"I'll get the papers back to Kathy in a day or so."

"A day or so? Are you crazy?"

"No, David. I have things to do."

"What? You're home all the time."

"I work now, remember?"

"You're not working tonight."

She didn't need this. "No, I'm not but I have kids to feed and bathe and a house to pack."

"Yeah, you're going to need to empty this place."

"I know that."

"You should've been out of here by now."

"I'm working on it." She was also working on keeping her temper.

"We need to sign. This guy wants to close as soon as possible. Next week if we're able." He leaned in. "He's even offering Kathy a bonus to get this all done quickly."

All the wine dropped to her stomach. She had to move but she had no money to hire movers. "David, can I talk to you outside. " She took his arm and they both stepped onto the porch, closing the door behind them. Every time she thought she'd hit bottom, life sent her a new low. "I hate to ask but is there any way that I can borrow the money to hire movers. I can pay you back as soon as we close."

He frowned. "I don't know. Steph won't like it."

"Then, don't tell her." She wanted to scream, cry and hide in her bed until all this was over or she died, whichever came first.

"I'm not keeping secrets from my wife."

"I'm sorry. Of course not. I shouldn't have said that." She took a deep breath, trying to calm herself. "I-I don't have the money and there's no way I can move everything myself even if I had a big enough car."

"Maybe, you shouldn't have wasted all your money on a new car." His eyes skimmed over the vehicle she'd borrowed from Terry. She'd left it in the driveway since Terry's friends had been moving the boxes from her garage. "That's a nice one."

"It isn't mine. My car is in the shop."

"An economy rental car wasn't good enough for you?"

"I'm not renting." She wished she could afford to do that. "A friend loaned it to me." She was so tired of explaining herself, but she needed the money.

"What friend? You don't have any friends."

That truth hit her like a punch in the gut. "You know what. Never mind." She turned and walked into the house.

"Mom, I'm hungry," said Peter

She was so close to falling apart but she couldn't. Her kids needed her. "Okay. I'll make you something."

It was almost ten when Maggie finally sat down. She'd pushed all her problems aside by keeping busy. It wasn't hard while feeding the kids, bathing them and then watching their favorite TV show with them, but now, they were asleep. The house was quiet and all her worries crashed down around her.

There was no way she was going to be able to move in a week or two. She could call Terry and agree to be his whore. She picked up her phone and tossed it on the floor before curling on the couch. She wasn't a whore and she wouldn't sleep with him for money. She couldn't.

There was a soft tap on the door.

She didn't want to answer it. This day had been nothing but bad.

There was another knock.

She had no idea who'd be coming over at this time. She walked to the window and peeked outside. Terry waited on the porch. He tapped on the door again. He'd come back. Her mood lightened, but she couldn't talk to him right now. She'd give in and then she'd never be able to forgive herself.

He pulled his phone from his pocket and tapped a button. Her phone rang. "Maggie, it's me. Come to the door. We need to talk."

She heard him through the open window but she didn't move. She'd talk to him later, but not now, not when she was this vulnerable.

"Damnit." He dialed her phone again. "Answer your phone or I'm going to ring the doorbell." He paused. "I'm sure your kids are asleep. I don't think you want me to wake them, especially the baby. They aren't so easy to get back to sleep."

She was going to kill him. She hurried to the door and opened it. "Go away."

CHAPTER 27: Terry

"You look like crap." Terry wanted to slap himself in the head. Once again, he'd uttered the exact wrong words.

"Thank you. Goodnight." Maggie started to close the door.

"Wait. I didn't mean it like that." He grabbed the handle.

"I've heard that before." She pulled on the door but was no match for his strength.

"We need to talk."

"No, we don't." She stopped trying to close the door but positioned herself in the doorway, making it apparent she didn't want him inside.

"Yes, we do." He stepped closer, her body drawing him near. He ran his finger across her cheek. "You've been crying."

"It's fine." She turned her face away but a tear slipped out when she blinked.

"It's not fine." He took her hands. "Tell me. I can help." He tugged her toward him and almost shouted hallelujah as she moved into his arms. "There, rabbit." He put one hand on her head and the other on her back, keeping her close.

"Stop calling me that," she mumbled against his chest.

"But you're my rabbit." He kissed the top of her head. "I didn't mean what I said earlier. Not the way you took it."

She stiffened. "So, exactly how did you mean it when you said I whored myself out for marriage?"

He took a deep breath. "I was angry and I don't understand why you won't let me help you."

"You want to give me money for sex." She pulled away from him.

He didn't want to but he let her go. "No, I want to take care of you."

"By giving me money and in return, I'll have sex with you."

He bit back replying, that's what she'd done with her ass-wipe of a husband. "Can I come inside so we can talk? Or do you want to have this conversation on your porch?"

"My kids are asleep."

"Let's not wake them by arguing out here."

"Go home." She looked away. "I really don't want to talk about this right now. I have other things to deal with."

"Like what?" He had no idea what'd happened. She should be happy because she no longer had to move.

"You're not going to leave, are you?"

"Not until we're good." And he'd fucked her. He'd been aching for her since he woke this morning.

"Garage." She stepped aside and pointed to the door through the kitchen.

"Garage?" That'd work. He could bend her over the car.

"It's farthest from the kids' rooms." She closed and locked the door behind her.

He headed across the kitchen and held the door to the

garage open. "Ladies first." That was his motto, at least as far as sex went.

She stepped through, turning on the light. Terry was quite disappointed when he realized that there wasn't a car in the garage. The car he'd loaned her had been in the driveway but his sex starved brain had imagined a different one in here. "Why is the car in the driveway?"

"We were supposed to move today, remember?"

"Ah, yeah." He preferred not to talk about earlier. "But why is it still out there?" And not in here for him to use for their fucking.

"I never went back outside. I'm sorry."

"I don't care." He walked over to her. Against the door would do, or she could bend, bracing herself on the counter. His dick rose, definitely liking the idea. He cupped her face. "I missed you." He lowered his head as he gripped her waist, pulling her closer. His lips were almost on hers.

"Don't." She turned away.

"Why?" He kissed her cheek. It wasn't what he wanted but it was a start.

"Stop it." She stepped away from him.

"I don't think you're a whore." He had to figure out how to fix this and how to keep his temper in check.

"I have to move." Her voice cracked.

"No, you don't."

She started pacing. "I do. Right away." She stopped and leaned against the counter.

He wanted to tell her to turn around and bend over, but his little rabbit wouldn't listen to him right now.

"I hate to ask this. I wouldn't if I had anyone else." Her lips quivered. She was upset and trying not to cry.

His libido calmed down. "What happened?" He moved over to her, taking her hands in his. "You can ask me anything. Anything at all." He'd do whatever she wanted if it kept her from crying.

"Can I borrow some money to hire movers? I'll pay you back as soon as the house sells and it won't be some unknown date in the future. We have an offer, a good one. It'll only be a week or so..." She was rambling.

"Stop. Stop." But she kept talking. This didn't make any sense. "Did you talk to your realtor?" He'd told Kathy to make sure that the owner, the person living in the house, knew that the buyer wouldn't be moving in for a while and that she could stay.

"No, but David told me. It's good news. It is." Her voice cracked.

"You should call your realtor."

She froze, mouth open a bit. "Why?"

"Talk to her. See if you can get the buyer to let you stay for a bit."

"Why bother? This guy is in a huge hurry to buy the house. He must need to move in right away."

"Maybe, maybe not." He had to tread carefully. "Just call your realtor."

"It's ten at night."

"So? Call her."

"I'll call her tomorrow. I have to give her the papers anyway."

"Call her tonight." He didn't want her worrying about moving. He wanted her happy and horny.

"My phone's in the house."

"So." He took her arm and led her out of the garage. "Where's your phone?"

"Living room."

He followed her into the other room and grabbed her phone from the floor, handing it to her. "Call her."

She frowned. "I don't know what good—"

"You'll sleep better if you know exactly when you need to be out of the house."

"I doubt that." But she scrolled through the contacts on her phone and then dialed, walking into the kitchen. She came back a moment later. "Went to voice mail."

"Did you leave a message?"

"Of course."

"I'm sure she'll call you back." He tapped his fingers against his leg. Damnit. That realtor needed to call. "I need to use the restroom."

"You know where it is."

"Yeah." He headed down the hallway, past the young boy's room. Memories of the evenings with his wife after their two kids had gone to sleep, flipped through his head. They'd wasted most of those nights, both of them going right to their computers. They should've fucked or just sat on the couch together and watched TV, anything to keep them connected. They'd been young and she'd been dealing with her homosexuality. He stepped into the bathroom and pulled his phone from his pocket.

He dialed Kathy and she answered on the first ring. "Terry, we're waiting—"

"Call Maggie."

"What?"

"You heard me. Call her back now." He hung up. She should've returned Maggie's call right away or better yet, answered the phone. Kathy had made a big mistake. He'd never use her services again. He flushed the toilet for good measure and left the bathroom.

Maggie was sitting on the couch, phone to her ear. "Really? You're kidding? Does David know? Oh. Uhm. Okay. I'll have the papers signed and to you tomorrow." She hung up the phone, her eyes wide with disbelief.

"Everything okay?' He moved to her side. She looked happy. If she'd trust him to handle this shit, he'd make sure she was always happy.

"Better than okay." A huge smile broke across her face.

"That's great. What did the realtor say?" He sat down next to her, close enough that his thigh pressed against hers. He put his hand on her knee and she didn't push it away. He rubbed his thumb across her leg, slowly sliding his hand upward.

"I don't need to borrow any money. Not from David and not from you."

He leaned down and kissed her neck. It was a small peck but the softness of her skin and the scent of vanilla made his dick stand at attention and then her words registered. "Borrow money from David?"

"Yeah." She tipped her head, not even aware that she was doing it, but he didn't kiss her. "I asked him if I could borrow the money to move." She frowned. "But he saw the car and decided that I didn't need any money."

"You asked your ex before you asked me?" He shifted away from her.

"Ah, yeah."

"Why the fuck would you do that?" He stood.

"Shhh." She got up and walked into the garage.

He followed, keeping his mouth shut until the door closed. "Why would you ask your ex for money before me? I get to take care of you, not him. He had his chance."

"I never asked you to take care of me and I don't need you to. I'm fine." She crossed her arms over her chest. "Better than fine."

"That you are." His eyes drifted down her body. He moved closer. "You need to listen closer to what I say."

"Do I?" Her eyes sparked with challenge, but her feet took a step back.

"Yes. I didn't say you needed me to take care of you." She did need him to look after her but saying that wouldn't get him what he wanted. "I said"—he stalked closer—"that I was the one who got to take care of you." She bumped into the wall and he lowered his head, so his lips pressed against her ear. "It's a privilege and a gift that you agreed to give to me." That, among other things.

"A gift? Giving someone money. Bailing them out of a world of mess? That's your idea of a gift." She tried to sound funny but her voice cracked.

"I do when it's you we're talking about." He kissed her ear and worked his way down her neck. "I want to take care of you. I want you to come to me with your problems so I can help you fix them."

"Why?" She tipped her head, her hands grasping his shirt.

"Because I like doing that. I need to do that."

"Be in charge?"

"Yes." His hands were at the button of her pants. "Fuck, Maggie. I need you." His lips found hers and he thrust into her mouth.

She kissed him back as she pulled at his shirt. He yanked it over his head, tossing it to the floor. He unfastened her pants and shoved them down, his hand stroking between her legs.

"Tell me you want this. That you want me." His finger slid beneath her underwear.

"Yes, please, Terry...Sir. Please." Her hands clutched at his back.

He pushed her shirt and bra up and his mouth latched onto a nipple. She moaned, her hips thrusting against his hand.

"Now, Maggie. I need to fuck you now."

"Yes." Her fingers moved to his pants, unbuttoning him and then unzipping. She reached inside, pulling him out. Her hand wrapped around his cock as he grabbed a condom from his pocket. He tore it open with his teeth and the breath hitched in his chest as her other hand caressed his balls.

"Fuck." He pushed his pants down and sild the condom on his dick. He yanked her legs up to his waist, positioning himself at her opening. "Tell me what you want."

"Sir...fuck me. Hard. Now. Please." She rocked her hips, rubbing against his length and he shoved inside in one hard push.

Her body squeezed his, making his knees shake from the pleasure. She was so tight and hot. He wanted nothing more than to fuck her hard like she'd asked but her breath hitched. She may want it, but she wasn't ready for a rough ride. His mouth moved to her breast, sucking and teasing her nipple. She moaned, her inner muscles clenching in need around his dick.

He slid out and back in, slower this time and she rocked with him. Her fingers digging into his shoulders.

"Come, Maggie. I need you to come for me." He was going to blow soon and ladies first. He shoved her hands over her head, pining her to the wall with his body and his cock. She rocked her hips and he bent his legs, shifting a bit until he found that spot deep inside her.

"Oh…oh." Her eyes flew open, locking with his.

That was it, her sweet spot. He increased his pace, shoving into her harder and faster but always making sure he hit that spot, over and over. Her pussy clenched around him trying to keep him inside, and he gritted his teeth as he withdrew, his thrusts getting shorter and faster, each time leaving her heaven less and less.

"Oh…god…oh…" She shuddered, clamping onto his dick so tight the air hissed through his teeth.

He bit down on her nipple and she screamed, her body rocking as she came. He covered her mouth with his hand. "Kids." He rasped in her ear.

She moaned, trembling around him. He thrust into her again and again as her body squeezed him. She was so tight, holding him so close. Lightning shot through his spine to his balls and he exploded, clasping her hips, holding her still so he could keep stroking into her until he was done.

He let her legs drop but kept her pinned to the door. He kissed her neck. "Fuck, rabbit. That was great."

"Hmm." Her hands skimmed down his back and she kissed his cheek. "If you want, you can come over every night after the kids go to bed." She nipped his ear.

"I want. I definitely want." He smiled against her neck.

CHAPTER 28: Terry

Terry was lying naked in Maggie's bed as she rushed around the room, pulling on clothes.

"Why can't your ex pick up the kids from school?" Davy was still sleeping. They had time for another fuck.

"He's busy." She slipped on her shoes.

"He's too busy now, but he'll be here almost as soon as you get back with them?" He sat up. "I'm sick of hiding in here." He'd spent the last several weeks sneaking into her house at night and sometimes in the afternoons. At first, the secrecy of it had been exciting but he was tired of the wham-bam-thank-you-ma'am relationship. He wanted to stay in bed with Maggie all night, not have her hurry him out so the kids didn't see him. "I get that you don't want your children seeing guys come in and out of your life, but it'd be good for them to know that not only men move on from failed marriages."

"Yes, I suppose it would be but not now." She walked over to him and kissed him softly. "You don't want to deal with the kids. You've said it yourself." She rested her hand on his chest.

"This is working. Let's not complicate it."

"Hmm." He took her hand and kissed it, not feeling at all happy about this. She was right. He had no interest in helping her raise her children but he wanted more than sneaking over for a quick, quiet fuck. "Fine, but this weekend you're all mine."

"Absolutely." Her hand drifted down his chest to between his legs. "And this is all mine."

He wrapped his hand around hers, making her squeeze his growing erection tighter. "Yes, it is."

"I'll be back soon." She straightened, her breathing irregular.

He watched her ass jiggle as she hurried out of the room, shutting the door behind her. He flopped back onto the bed. He'd love to take a little nap, but if the kids snuck in here for some reason, she wouldn't be happy if they caught him naked in her bed. He stretched and went into the bathroom. He had time for a quick shower before she got back.

Terry was sitting on the bed answering emails when the bedroom door opened.

Maggie leaned against it and sighed. "They're gone."

He tossed his phone on the nightstand, his cock already rising. "Take off your clothes."

Her breathing increased, causing her breasts to rise and fall. He wanted to bury his face between them and never come out. She pulled her T-shirt off and his mouth went dry. He'd never tire of seeing her body—so lush and round, the kind of body a man could savor.

Her hands moved to her pants.

"No. Your bra. I want to see your tits."

Her face flushed. He wasn't sure if it was excitement or still a modicum of embarrassment over his language.

Her hands went behind her back and unhooked her bra, holding it in place for a moment before letting it drop.

"Fuck, Maggie. You're so beautiful."

Her eyes lowered.

"One day, I'll make you believe it." He pulled off his shirt as she took off her pants and underwear.

She stood naked at the door, waiting for his command. His little rabbit was learning fast.

"Come here."

She moved toward him, her hips swaying. He couldn't wait to plunge inside her, feel all that soft skin under him and surrounding him. She stopped at the edge of the bed. He swung his legs off the side and leaned toward her, grabbing her nipple and rubbing it between his thumb and finger.

"I love your body." He kissed between her breasts.

She held his head, her fingers playing with his hair. His mouth moved across her breast, licking and sucking her taut little peak. She moaned, her hand trailing down his chest to his pants.

He grabbed her wrist. "Not yet, rabbit. I'll tell you when I want you to undress me."

"Sorry, Sir."

He kissed her palm.

"I want you, Sir. I've been thinking about this since I got out of bed."

He smiled and leaned forward flicking her nipple with his tongue. "Good but I want to hear you." His hand trailed between her legs. "I'm going to make you scream. Over and over until you can't talk."

Her body shivered under his touch.

He leaned back, stretching out on the bed. "Come here."

She crawled up, positioning herself over his cock.

He stared up at her, smiling. "No. Come here." He motioned her forward.

"Terry?" She looked at him confused.

"Put that sweet pussy over my face."

"Oh, I-I can't." Her cheeks flushed scarlett.

"You will." His eyes locked with hers. "Come here. Now."

She took a deep breath and crawled off him moving across the bed. His hands caressed down her back to her ass.

"Terry, please." She stopped near his shoulder. "I can't. This is embarrassing."

"Rabbit, put your pussy over my face or I won't let you come tonight." He slapped her ass. "Maybe, all weekend."

"You wouldn't."

He raised a brow. "Don't tempt me. It'll be a very long and frustrating weekend for you if you don't do as you're told." Plus, it'd screw up his plans because he wanted, no needed, to hear her scream her release.

She frowned down at him.

"If you don't like it—"

"I don't."

He laughed. "You haven't even tried it yet." His hand trailed up the inside of her leg and she unconsciously shifted, giving him access. His finger skimmed along her slit. She was already swollen and wet for him. "I want to taste you. It's been so long." She made too much noise when he went down on her for them to do that while the kids slept.

"Like this." She started to lie back, opening her legs.

"No." He squeezed her thigh. "You. Over my face." He leaned up and kissed her leg. "If you don't like it, we can stop. All you have to do is say your safeword."

"I don't—"

"Maggie, for me." That was his favorite thing about her. She was so giving, she never refused him this request.

"Okay, but I'm not going to like it."

He grinned up at her as he relaxed on the bed. "We'll see about that."

CHAPTER 29: Maggie

Maggie didn't want to do this. She loved having Terry go down on her, but this...She straddled his face, her cheeks burning as she stared at him. His eyes were locked on her pussy and she wanted to cover herself or shove her head under her pillow.

"Come here." His voice was a dark rasp that she couldn't disobey.

She lowered and he inhaled sharply.

"You smell so fucking good." His hands were on her thighs, pulling her downward. "Put your hands on the headboard." She did as he said. "Now, come here so I can taste you."

She stared at the wall as she lowered herself, her body stiff. This wasn't normal. It wasn't right and then his tongue was there, a tickle of motion and heat. Her fingers tightened on the headboard and she shifted downward, not caring that this was wrong, only caring about the pleasure. His tongue flicked again, teasing her. She bit her lip, trying not to cry out–habit from all those wonderful nights and afternoons sneaking around while the kids slept or Davy napped.

"I want to hear you." His lips pressed against her opening and his deep voice vibrated through her.

She couldn't help it. She shifted lower. He smiled between her legs and she wanted to die, but not if it meant moving because his tongue was playing along her slit, dipping in and lapping at her. His hands tightened on her thighs, holding her in place but she wasn't going anywhere, except maybe lower. His lips closed over her tiny bundle of nerves and sucked as he shoved a finger inside her.

She moaned, low and long, her body rocking to the rhythm of his finger. "Oh...oh...Terry."

"Don't you come." He eased off her clit, licking her in long, lazy strokes.

She dropped her head against the headboard. "Please, Sir. I want to come. I need to come."

"No."

"Shit," she mumbled. He was trying to kill her.

His tongue joined his finger and he stroked her inside before moving to her labia, teasing and playing. The deep thrust of his finger and the rough rasp of his tongue sent spirals of pleasure ricocheting through her. She rocked against his face, whimpering. She needed to come. She was so close. She couldn't wait. She lifted one hand from the headboard, her fingers slipping between her legs. All she needed was a little touch.

"No, you don't." He shoved her hand away. "Hold the headboard or I stop."

"Oh, god. Please, don't stop." She grabbed the headboard. That'd be worse than not coming, at least she was still close, still had pleasure zinging through her.

"Do you like this, rabbit?" He flicked her clit.

"Yes."

"I was right, wasn't I?"

He was such an arrogant ass, but he wasn't wrong. "Yes." She bit her lip as he pushed another finger inside of her.

"You're going to trust me from now on, right?" He sucked her clit.

"Yes. Yes." Her pussy throbbed for release.

His fingers moved faster and faster while the pressure from his mouth increased.

"God, Terry...Sir. I'm coming. I...please." She took great gasping breaths, fighting her orgasm, waiting on his permission.

He let up on her clit. "Come for me, Maggie."

His lips were back on her, hot and wet. Her hips thrust toward him, seeking release. He bit down gently, sending her over the edge. She screamed as her body bucked, rocking against his face.

CHAPTER 30: Terry

Terry continued to lick Maggie's pussy and stroke her with his fingers until her spasms stopped. He kissed each thigh and looked up at her. She had her head resting on the headboard, her breathing still erratic.

"My turn." He lifted her leg and rolled to the side. She started to move toward him. "Stay right where you are."

"I thought..." Her eyes dropped to his pants and she licked her lips.

His cock, already hard and aching, must've grown another inch. She gave great head, always eager and willing to suck his dick, but that'd have to wait. "Later. I'd never last and I want to make you scream while my cock plunges inside you."

He stood, removing his pants. He was so fucking glad they weren't using condoms anymore. She'd been tested and put on birth control. He was regularly tested for the Club, even though he hadn't spent much time there lately, except in the back office playing cards with Ethan while he waited for her kids to go to sleep.

He crawled back on the bed, his dick in his hands. "Face the wall and hold the headboard.

She did, shifting a little and spreading her legs for him.

He caressed her butt cheeks. They were soft and firm. "I love your ass." He swatted it and she moaned. She didn't even give him a squeak of protest any longer. He kissed her neck as his hand drifted between her thighs. "You're so slick and wet. I'm going to fuck you now."

"Yes, Sir. Please."

He wrapped his hand around her neck, pulling back her head so his mouth could explore while his other hand lined his dick up with her slit. "You ready?"

"Yes," she whimpered.

"Tell me what you want." He loved making her say it. She was getting more used to talking dirty but she still flushed a pretty pink.

"I want you, Sir. Your cock."

"Where do you want it?" He teased her, letting the hard head of his shaft press against her clit.

"Oh, yes. There."

"Here." He rubbed against her tiny nub again. "Or here?" He pushed the tip in just a little, gritting his teeth to keep from sheathing himself fully. She was so fucking hot and wet. He could slide in and she'd grip him like a second skin.

"There. Please." She pushed against him and he bit her neck, making her moan.

"Hold still." He nipped her ear as he pushed in a little more, going as slow as he could to savor every moment and each whimper he drew from her lips. "You like my big cock, don't you?"

"Yes, Sir. Please. I want your big cock."

"I'm giving it to you." He slid inside a little more, his arms shaking with the desire to plunge into her warmth.

"Faster, Sir. Please. More."

Her phone rang and she glanced at the table.

"Ignore it."

"It could be the kids."

"Fucking, ignore it." Nothing would stop him now. Nothing. He sheathed himself and she moaned. It was low and filled with pleasure, making his balls tighten. "Fuck, Maggie." She felt so good wrapped around him, going slow was over. Her whimpers and moans hurtled him toward the edge. His hips rocked, shoving inside her faster and deeper. His other hand slipped around her waist and pressed against her abdomen. "You need to come, Maggie. Come on my cock." He thrust harder, shifting until he found that spot that drove her wild.

She writhed against him but he held her in place. He bit her shoulder as his balls tightened. She screamed, her body clamping down on him. He shoved into her and grunted against her neck as he found his release.

CHAPTER 31: Terry

Terry wrapped his arm around Maggie and lifted her, dropping her onto the bed and falling beside her. He pulled her into his arms, spooning her. Even flaccid, he loved the way her ass cradled his dick.

He kissed her neck. "As soon as I can move, we should go get something to eat."

"Hmm." Her hand held his against her breast.

"Then, we'll go to my place." He kissed her ear. "I want to tie you to my bed. Your hands and legs. You'll be open for me. Unable to move."

She stilled.

"You'll like it. Trust me." He kissed the back of her head.

"Okay."

His heart almost burst. This was a big step for her, for anyone. The first time being completely restrained was always risky. "Thank you." He leaned over, his lips finding hers.

The phone rang again.

"Ignore it." He loosened his grip, knowing she wouldn't and

he didn't blame her. It could be her kids

"I can't."

"I know." He rolled onto his back as she leaned over to the nightstand and grabbed her phone.

"Hello?" Maggie was quiet a moment. "Uh, can't you find anyone else? No. Okay. I'll be there." She pressed a button and put the phone down.

"That didn't sound like it had anything to do with the kids."

"It didn't."

"Then, I must've misheard you." He grabbed her and pinned her beneath him. "Because you aren't going anywhere tonight except with me." He kissed her and her arms wrapped around him but she shifted, ending the kiss too quickly.

"I'm sorry. It was work." Her fingers played in his hair. "I have to go in. Nancy's kids are sick."

"Too bad for Nancy." He kissed down her neck to that spot on her shoulder that made her crazy.

"Stop." She sighed, her body softening under him but she pushed on his chest. "Let me up."

"No." He pressed more firmly down on her. "You promised me this weekend." He sounded like a kid but he didn't care. He felt like one—sneaking around for quickies, never being able to be with her when he wanted, always waiting on her kids to fall asleep or for her to not be at work.

"I know and I'm sorry." She touched his cheek. "I really am, but I have to go to work."

"No, you don't." He wasn't giving up that easily. He had plans for this weekend—wicked, glorious plans. He kissed her neck, nibbling and sucking. Her legs slipped open and he smirked as she grabbed his hair and tugged.

"Terry, stop. I have to go." Her other hand pushed on his chest.

"But you don't." He snatched it and kissed her palm.

"I do. I answered and now they're expecting me."

"And I was expecting to fuck you all weekend."

Her cheeks flushed. "I can still see you after work."

"Not good enough." He kissed her lips, letting his tongue dip inside. "I want all weekend. You. At my house. Naked. Willing. Whenever and however I want." He was hard and ready just thinking about it.

She pulled away. "I'm sorry but I have to go." She shoved on him. "Let me up." Her eyes sparkled mischievously. "I'll make it up to you."

"No."

"Terry, get off me."

"Damnit, Maggie." His jaw tensed but he rolled to the side.

"I'm sorry." She crawled out of bed. "I need this job."

"Bullshit."

"What?" She spun toward him.

"You closed on the house. You have money."

She grabbed her housecoat, wrapping it around herself. "That money has to last."

"Please. It's a considerable sum." He knew how much he paid for the house. Thanks to Patrick and his security firm, Terry knew exactly how much Maggie and her husband had owed and exactly what they each received from the sale.

"Yes, but I still have to move and—"

"No, you don't."

"I do. Not right away, but the owner is going to eventually want to move in."

"Worry about that when it happens."

"I can't wait until then." She gave him a dirty look as she headed for the shower. "You don't understand because you're rich, but the money for my house and my job is all the money I have or am going to get. I can't afford to lose this job and blow through the money for the house. I just can't."

"That is such bullshit." He got out of bed, his dick bobbing in front of him. "You're getting more than enough money to watch this place." He was paying her plenty to live in her own house. She did not have to work.

She stopped in the doorway and slowly turned. "How do you know about that?"

Shit. Fuck and double damn. His mind tumbled over itself but the only thing he could find was, "You told me." He was glad it didn't come out like a question.

"I did not."

"You did." He had to bluff his way through this.

"No. I didn't. The only ones who know are me, Kathy and…" Her eyes widened.

He prayed she thought he was fucking Kathy.

"You." She looked around her room. "You bought my house."

He might as well come clean. "I told you, I'd take care of you."

Her mouth dropped open and then closed with a clank. "Get out."

"Maggie." He strode toward her.

"Don't come near me."

He kept walking. He had to touch her. He could make her understand, but he had to be touching her.

"Stop." She clutched the housecoat at her throat, as if to protect herself from him. "Red."

He stopped immediately. She'd used the one word he'd hoped to never hear pass her lips. He had to fix this—get to Yellow, or better yet, Green. "Listen to me. This is a good thing."

"Good?" Tears filled her eyes.

"Yes. Good." His little rabbit was ready to bolt. He had to convince her. "For you. For your kids. For everyone." He moved a little closer.

"You did it." She laughed, a hurt, hollow sound. "You made me your whore."

"Don't start that again." They'd talked and argued about that way too much.

"I didn't. You did."

"No. I took care of you. That's all."

"You paid for me and I..." She shook her head. "I was such a fool. You knew. That night after you called me a whore you...I should've known. You told me to call Kathy. You knew I didn't have to move because you'd bought the house." She backed away. "I have to leave. I can't stay here." Her eyes darted around the room. "I have to re-pack everything. I lost the lease on the apartment."

"Shhh. You don't have to move." Terry pulled her to him.

"Let me go." She wrapped her arms around his waist, resting her face on his chest.

"Shhh. Baby. It's okay."

"But it's not." She pushed away from him. "Don't you understand? Now, everything between us is different."

"It's not." Why couldn't she see that he was taking care of her. He was doing exactly what a good dom does for his sub.

"It is. You own the house. You can kick me out." She started pacing. "If I don't do what you say, do whatever you want, you can evict me and my kids."

"You know, I'd never do that." It was like she'd slapped him.

"Do I?" She smiled, but her lips quivered. "I barely know you."

That hurt more than it should.

"All I know about you is that you'll stop at nothing to have things your way. No matter what. No matter how it makes someone else feel. No matter who you hurt." Her eyes flashed with anger as tears streamed down her cheeks.

"Who did I hurt? Tell me." He'd never hurt any of his subs. Never.

"Me, Terry. You hurt me." She turned and walked into the bathroom, closing the door behind her.

"Fuck that, Maggie." He stormed to the door, hitting it with the palm of his hand. "Oh, I'm so sorry, I threw a fucking load of money at you so you wouldn't have to worry about moving. So, your kids could stay in a nice place. So, you didn't have to work. Yeah, I'm a horrible guy."

The door flew open. "Don't you dare pretend you did any of this for me or my kids." She poked his chest. "You did this for you. So, you'd win. So, you'd get what you want."

"Maggie." He grabbed her finger.

"Goodbye, Terry." She pulled free and slammed the bathroom door.

Fury raged through him. He didn't need this shit. He pulled on his underwear and pants. He didn't deserve this shit. He grabbed his shirt. "You know what?" She didn't answer. He didn't expect her to. "Fuck you, Maggie." He put on his shoes and strode to the door. "Call me when you're ready to apologize."

"Go to hell," she yelled.

"I'm already there." He slammed the bedroom door, made his way down the hallway and slammed the door to the garage. He got into his car, slammed that door too but none of it made him feel one tiny bit better.

Get the next part of the story here or keep reading for an excerpt.

https://ellisoday.com/books/his-submission/

PART THREE – HIS SUBMISSION

CHAPTER 1: Terry

Terry sat in the business part of the Club, not in the office with Ethan. It was Saturday night, over twenty-four hours since the fight, and Maggie still hadn't called him. They were done. Finished. He tossed back another drink.

"Hey, Ethan said you were in here." Nick sat next to him at the bar.

"Yep." He waved his hand and the bartender filled his glass. "Glenlivet for him too." He nodded at Nick.

"Thanks," said Nick as the bartender returned with his

drink.

"What are you doing here?" asked Terry. "Finally see the light and realize men weren't created to be monogamous."

"No, nothing like that." Nick smiled. "Sarah's out with her sister and Annie."

"Does that mean Patrick's coming here too?" He took a gulp of his drink. "That's cause for celebration."

"No. Patrick is upstairs with Ethan. We're getting ready for poker. You should join us."

"Later. First, you guys should come down and we can find us some women. Just like the old days."

"Not interested."

"You make me embarrassed to be a man." His eyes roamed the Club. "There are a ton of beautiful, eager, horny women and you want to hide upstairs and play poker."

"Ethan said you and Maggie had another fight. Come upstairs and talk to us. Maybe, we can help."

"I don't need your fucking help." He tossed back his drink. "I need to get laid." His eyes landed on Desiree, one of Ethan's newer employees. "By her."

The bartender filled his drink.

"Don't do this."

He tipped his glass in the young woman's direction. "She's exquisite."

Nick's eyes roamed over her. "She is, but she's not worth it."

He knew what Nick meant but decided to play dumb. "I have more money than I can spend. She's worth whatever price she wants."

"That's not what I meant and you know it." Nick turned to

him. "Don't throw away what you have with Maggie over one stupid fight."

"I'm not." His chest tightened and his stomach twisted, adding another knot to his tangled mess of emotions. "It's over between us."

"Only if you want it to be or if you do this."

"You don't know shit." He gulped down the drink and ordered another. "I thought she was special but she's not going to work."

"Just because she won't take your money? That's the stupidest thing I've ever heard. You, of all people, should appreciate that about her."

"I don't give a damn about the money."

"Then what is it?"

"She doesn't trust me."

"Are you sure? I thought that about Sarah too and she did trust me. She just had to deal with some issues of her own."

"I'm sure." He was done with this conversation. It was bringing him down and he'd spent a fortune and many hours drinking his way to happy. "And, I'm sure that I'm going to fuck that exotic, young woman over there."

"Terry, come upstairs. Don't make this decision when you're drunk."

That was the only time he could because when he was sober, he only wanted Maggie. "Nope. I need pussy." He stood.

Nick grabbed his arm. "And you can have it, later. Sober up first." He looked at Ethan's new hire. "She'll appreciate you more if you're not sloppy drunk when you fuck her."

"I'm not a novice. I know how to please a woman drunk or sober." He jerked free and staggered a bit, grabbing onto a chair to steady himself. "Go. Play poker. I've got plans."

He made his way across the bar. The young woman watched him, a hint of a smile on her full, gorgeous lips.

He stopped by her side. "May I buy you a drink?"

"Absolutely." She smiled at him.

"You're stunning." He plopped down next to her, waving the bartender over.

"Thank you." She turned toward the bartender. "Soda water with lime."

"Not drinking?" He couldn't take his eyes from her. She was the most beautiful woman he'd ever seen with jet-black hair, pale complexion and blue eyes. She could be Irish but the tip to her eyes spoke of something else in her blood.

"I've already had two and I don't like to get drunk."

"Really?" Most of the women here drank quite a bit. Actually, so did the men.

"I find a little is better." She took a sip and his eyes locked on her luscious, red lips.

"Fuck, you're beautiful."

"Thank you." She smiled at him again. "You're not so bad yourself."

"Let's go to a room."

"Wow. You move fast."

"You should be used to that." He caressed the bracelet she wore, telling everyone that she was an employee.

"I expect it from some, but I didn't from you." She studied him.

He was surprised by the intelligence in her gaze. Most beautiful women who worked her weren't stupid, but they weren't this smart either. "Why is that?"

"I've been watching you and you didn't seem interested in anything but your drink until your friend arrived."

"I was taking my time." His fingers trailed along the skin of her arm. It was soft and firm but not as soft as Maggie. He pushed the thought away. "Deciding who I wanted to spend my *time* with tonight." And his money.

"I'm honored."

"But are you accepting?" He was pretty sure she was being sarcastic but not positive. Maybe, he shouldn't have drank so much but fuck, he'd needed it to forget Maggie. He leaned down so his breath caressed her ear. "I'll make it well worth your time."

"Hmm. I don't usually go anywhere, let alone to a private room, with a man I've just met."

"You work here." That was exactly what Ethan's employees did.

She laughed. It was a tinkling, melodious sound that went straight to his balls and caused his dick, which had been sleeping, to wake up.

"I do but that doesn't mean I have to accompany everyone who asks...or anyone who asks. Ethan made that very clear."

"I understand that, but I never met anyone who turned down a handful of cash." Except Maggie. It was just his luck to pick the one woman here who also wasn't interested in his money. Someone must've put a curse on him.

"Now, you have." She held out her hand. "Desiree."

"Terry." He shook her hand and ordered another drink. He'd put up with enough of Maggie's crap he wasn't about to do it with this young woman. "So, Desiree, this is how it's going to work." He stared at her. "I'm going to finish this drink and by the time I'm done, you're either going to agree to go into a private room with me or I'm going to walk away and find someone who isn't so particular." He held up his glass. "Understand?"

"Absolutely." She smiled and clinked her glass against his. "May I ask you some questions to help me decide?"

"Sure." He couldn't blame her. She'd want to know what he wanted but right now he wasn't sure. Part of him wanted to fuck someone, anyone, to make him forget Maggie, but another part wanted to tie someone up and take out his frustrations on her. That settled it. Punishing someone when angry was never a good idea. "I'm a dom but I don't want anything rough, not tonight."

"Why is that?" She seemed genuinely interested.

A few people milled about nearby. "Can we go to the back? Same rules. I finish my drink and you decide to stay or go." He looked around. "Too many ears around here."

Her blue eyes sharpened as she studied him.

"I swear. I won't touch you, unless you agree to stay."

"Okay."

He stood. "At least someone trusts me," he muttered under his breath as he offered her his hand.

"Excuse me?" She put her hand in his.

"Nothing." He led her across the room, his other hand on the small of her back. She was short and curvaceous but thinner than Maggie. Her ass wouldn't be as soft. It wouldn't cradle his dick as well. He took another gulp of his drink. He needed to get Maggie out of his fucking head.

Find out what happens next.

See below for a sneak peek of Interviewing for her Lover (Nick and Sarah's story) and The Voyeur (Patrick and Annie's story). They're both free on all ebook retailers. You can get the entire Six Nights of Sins series (Nick and Sarah's six nights of kinky fun) for free. A thank you gift for joining my newsletter.

Here's What You Get When You
Join My Readers' Group

Win Before You Can Buy
Exclusive Giveaways
Free Books
Sneak Peeks

Go to my website or email me for details:

https://www.EllisODay.com

authorellisoday@gmail.com

Interviewing For Her Lover

CHAPTER 1: SARAH

"Do I have to take off my clothes?" Sarah tugged on
the hem of her black dress. It was shorter and lower cut in
the front than she normally wore, but the Viewing was
about finding a man for sex and according to Ethan men
liked to look.

"No." Ethan turned her away from the door and forced her to look at him. "You don't have to do anything you don't want to do."

She stared into his blue eyes. Why couldn't he be interested in her? She'd only met with him five or six times, but she trusted him. He ran his business, La Petite Mort Club, very professionally and he was gorgeous with his sandy brown hair, strong cheekbones and vibrant blue eyes. Sex between them would be good. Easy. He was attractive and...not for her. She didn't want decent sex or good sex, she wanted mind blowing, screaming orgasms and that wouldn't happen between him and her because there was no chemistry, no attraction.

"Listen to me." He moved his hands to her shoulders and gave her a gentle shake. "You aren't selling yourself to the highest bidder. You're looking for a partner. One who'll"—he grinned—"turn you on in ways you can't even imagine."

She glanced at the door where the men waited. Waited for her. Waited to decide if they wanted to fuck her. "I'm a bit nervous."

"About what?"

This was embarrassing but she'd been honest with him up to this point. She'd had to be. He was helping her...had helped her to choose the five men in the other room. "What if none of them…"

"They will want you." He touched her chin, turning her face toward him. "A few of them may back out after this but not because they don't want you."

"Yeah, right."

"I'm only going to say this once. You're beautiful and different, unique."

"That's not necessarily a good thing." She had long legs and a nice body—trim and firm—but with her auburn hair and green eyes she was cute at best, not gorgeous. The men she'd chosen were all rich, good looking and powerful. They could have anyone they wanted.

"It's exactly what they want, or most of them anyway." He took her hand and led her closer to the door.

She leaned on his arm, hating these shoes. She should've stuck with her flats but Ethan had given her a list of what she should wear and high heels were on the top. She'd found the smallest heels in the store and by Ethan's look when he'd first seen her she might've been better off going barefoot. He'd met her at the private entrance and his gaze had been appreciating as it'd skimmed over her dress, until he got to her feet. Then he'd frowned and shook his head.

"Finding the right men for you wasn't easy." He stopped at the door.

"Thanks a lot." She shifted away from him, his words hurting a little. She hadn't been sure of her appeal to the opposite sex in a long time, not since the early years with Adam.

"It's not because you aren't beautiful but because you want to be dominated and you want to dominate—"

"I do not want to dominate." All she could picture was a woman in black leather with a whip and that wasn't her, not at all.

"If you say so." He smiled a little. "But, you do want to lead the scene. Right? Because that's what—"

"Yes." Her face was red. She could feel it. She didn't want to talk about her fantasies again. It'd been embarrassing enough the first time, but he'd had to know what she wanted to compile a list of candidates.

"Most at the club are either doms or subs. Very few are switches." His eyes raked over her. "That's what's so special about you. You want it all and…that's what made choosing these men difficult."

He'd given her a selection of twenty-two men who might be interested in what she wanted. She'd narrowed it down to seven. Two had been uninterested when he'd approached. That'd left her with the five who'd see her in person for the first time tonight, but she wouldn't see them. That'd come after the Viewing when she interviewed any who were still interested.

"Remember what you want. This is your deal. You call the shots. At least a little." He kissed her forehead. "But don't refuse to give them anything. You don't want a submissive."

"No." That didn't turn her on at all and she only had eight weeks. One night each week for two months before she'd go back to her lonely life, her lonely bed, dreaming of Adam.

"You can do this." He pulled a flask from his jacket and unscrewed the lid. "For courage."

"Thanks." She took a large swallow, the brandy too thick and sweet for her taste but it was better than nothing.

"Now, go find your lover."

She laughed a little but sadness swept through her. There'd be no love between this man and herself. This would be sex, fucking. That's all. The only man she'd ever love, her only lover, was dead. This was purely physical. "Thank you again." She stood on tip-toe and kissed his cheek. He may be gorgeous and run a sex club but he was a good man, a good friend.

She turned and opened the door and walked into the room, trying to stay balanced on these stupid heels. Men wouldn't find them so attractive if they had to wear them. The room was dark except for one light highlighting a small platform. That was for her. She stepped up onto the small stage. The room was silent but they were there, above her, hidden behind the one-way mirrors, watching and deciding if they wanted to take the next step—to eventually take her.

She stared into the blackness of the room. It wasn't huge but its emptiness made it seem vast. She glanced upward, the light making her squint and she quickly stared back into the darkness. This was arranged for them to see her. That was it. She'd get no glimpse of them yet. She'd seen their pictures, chosen them but meeting them in person would be different. A picture couldn't tell her their smell or the sound of their voices.

She tugged at her dress where it hugged her hips, wishing the questions would start, but there was only silence. She shifted, the heels already killing her feet. Ethan hadn't liked them and if they weren't going to impress, she might as well take them off. She moved to the back of the stage, leaned against the wall and removed her shoes. As she returned to the center of the stage a man spoke, his voice loud and commanding almost echoing throughout the room.

"Don't stop there. Take off your dress."

She bent, placing her shoes on the floor. That wasn't part of the deal. She wasn't going to undress in front of five men, only one. Only the one she chose. She straightened. "No."

"What?" He was surprised and not happy.

"I said no. That's not part of the Viewing."

"I want to see what I'm getting."

She stared up toward the windows, squinting a little. She couldn't tell from where the voice had come. The speaker system made it sound as if it were coming from God himself. "And you will if I pick you."

Another man laughed.

"It's not funny. She's disobedient," said the man with the loud voice.

"Not always. I can be obedient." These men liked to be in control but sometimes, so did she.

"Will you raise your dress? Just a little," asked another voice.

"Didn't you see enough in the photos?" She'd applied a few months ago for this one-time contract. She'd been excited and nervous when she'd received the acceptance email with an appointment for a photography session. She'd never had her picture professionally taken, since she didn't count school portraits or the ones her parents had had done at JCPenny's. She'd been anxious and a little turned on imaging wearing her new lingerie in front of a strange man, so she'd been disappointed to find the photographer was an elderly woman, but the lady had put her at ease and the photos had turned out better than she'd expected. She glanced up at the mirrors, hoping she wasn't disappointing all the men. That'd be too embarrassing.

"Those were…nice, but I'd like to see the real thing before deciding if you're worth my time."

She raised a brow. "You can always leave." She shouldn't antagonize him. She was sure the bossy man had already decided against committing to this agreement. Disobedience didn't appeal to him. That left four. If she didn't pick any of them, she could go through the process again, but she didn't think she would.

The man chuckled slightly. "I know that, but I haven't decided I don't want to fuck you. Not yet, anyway."

The word, so harsh and vulgar excited her. It was the truth. That was what she, what they were all deciding. Who'd get to fuck her. It was what she wanted, what she'd agreed to do, and as much as she dreaded it, she wanted it.

She was tired of being alone. She missed having a man inside her—his tongue and fingers and cock.

"Do any of you have any questions?" She clasped her dress at her waist and slowly gathered it upward, displaying more and more of her long legs. She ran. They were in shape. The men would like them.

"Lower your top," said the same man who'd told her to take off her dress.

She didn't like him. If he didn't back out, she'd have Ethan remove him from her list. He was too commanding. He'd never allow her to be in control.

"I don't know if he's done looking at my legs yet." She continued raising the dress until her black and green lace panties were almost exposed.

"Very nice and thank you," said the polite man.

"You're welcome." This man might work. She shifted the dress up another inch before dropping it, giving them a glance at her panties.

"Now, your top," said the bossy guy.

She lowered her spaghetti string off one shoulder, letting the dress dip, but not enough to show anything besides the side of her bra.

"More," he said.

"No." She raised the strap, covering herself. She

didn't like this man and wished he'd leave. She'd kick him out but that wasn't part of the process and they were very firm about their rules at this club.

"He got to see your pussy. Why don't I get to see your tits?"

"You got to see as much as he did." She was ready to move on. She bent and picked up her shoes. "If there's nothing else, gentleman, we can set up times for the interview process."

"Turn around," said another man.

It was a command, but she didn't mind. There was a politeness to his order and something about the texture of his voice caused an ache between her thighs. There was a caress in his tone but with an edge and a promise of a good hard fuck.

"Are you going to obey?" His words were whisper soft and smooth.

"Yes." That was going to be part of this too. Her commanding and him commanding. She dropped her shoes and turned.

"Raise you dress again."

She looked over her shoulder at where she imagined he sat watching her.

"Please." There was humor in his tone.

She smiled and slowly gathered the dress upward. She stopped right below the curve of her bottom.

"More. Please." There was a little less humor in his voice.

She wanted to show him her ass. She wanted to show that voice everything but not with the others around. This would be just her and one man, one stranger. That was one of her rules. "No. Only if you're picked do you get to see any more of me than you have." She dropped her dress, grabbed her shoes and walked off the stage and out the door.

She was going to have sex with a stranger. She was going to live out her fantasies for eight nights with a man she didn't know and would never really know, but she wasn't going to lose who she was. She'd keep her honor and her dignity which meant she had to pick a man who'd agree with her rules.

Get your free ebook copy.

http://books2read.com/u/3nYKo6

The Voyeur

CHAPTER 1: ANNIE

Annie finished making the bed and gathered the sheets from the floor, keeping them as far away from her body as possible. These sex rooms were disgusting and Ethan was a jerk making her work as a maid. She almost had her Bachelor's Degree in Culinary Arts, but he'd refused to hire her for the kitchen—too many men in the kitchen. The only job he'd give her at La Petite Mort Club was as a maid and unfortunately, she needed the money too badly to refuse.

She stuffed the dirty sheets into the cart and hurried out the door. She had almost thirty minutes before she had to be at the next "sex room." She hid the cart in a closet and darted down a back hallway, staying clear of the cameras. Julie, the woman who supervised the daytime maids, was a real bitch. If she were caught sneaking away from her duties, she'd be assigned to the orgy rooms every day. Right now, they all took turns cleaning that nightmare. She swore they should get hazard pay to even go in those rooms.

She slipped through a doorway and hurried to the one-way mirror. She stared at the couple in the next room. From her first day here, she'd been curious about the activities at the club. She was twenty-four and wasn't a virgin but she'd never, ever done some of these things.

The woman in the room below was tied to a table, legs spread and wearing some sort of leather outfit that left her large breasts free and her crotch exposed. She had shaved her pussy and her pink lower lips were swollen and glistening from her excitement. The man strolled around the table as if he had all night. He still had his pants on but had removed his shirt. His arms and chest were well defined but he had a slight paunch. His erection tented his pants and Annie felt wetness pool between her legs. She had no idea why watching this turned her on but it did.

Ever since she'd accidentally barged in on that guy and girl in the Interview room, she couldn't stop watching.

The man below ran his hand up the woman's inner thigh, glancing over her pussy. The woman thrust her hips upward and Annie ran her own hand between her legs. The man's mouth moved but Annie couldn't hear anything and then he slapped the woman across the thigh hard enough to leave a red mark. Annie jumped. She wasn't into that, but she couldn't stop watching the woman's face. At first, it'd contorted in pain but then it'd morphed into pleasure. The man hit her again and then bent, kissing the red welts— running his tongue across them as his fingers squeezed her nipple.

Annie clutched her thighs together, searching for some relief. Her panties were soaked. It wouldn't take but a few strokes to make her come. She started to slide her hand into her pants.

"Having fun?" asked a deep voice from behind her.

She spun around, her heart dropping into her stomach. "Ah…I was just finishing cleaning in here." Damn, she should've closed the door but she hadn't expected anyone in this area. The rooms were off limits on this floor until tonight and she was the only one assigned to clean here.

He shut the door and locked it before strolling toward her. She'd seen him around the Club, but more than that she remembered him from the military photos her brother, Vic, had sent to her. She carried one of the three of them—Vic, Ethan and this guy, Patrick—in her purse. He'd been attractive in the picture, but now that he was older and in person he was gorgeous. He had dark green eyes, brown hair and a perfect body. He stopped so close to her his chest almost brushed against her breasts. She was pretty sure it would if she inhaled deeply. She really wanted to take that deep breath and feel his hard chest against her breasts.

"Don't let me stop you from enjoying the show."

"I…I wasn't. I should go." She started to walk past him but he grabbed her hand.

His grip was warm and strong but loose enough that she could pull free if she wanted. She didn't. Even though she only knew him from her brother's pictures and letters, she'd had many fantasies about him when she'd been in high school. Her gaze dropped to the front of his pants and her mouth almost watered. He was definitely interested. She dragged her eyes up his body, stopping on his face. He smiled at her.

"There's nothing to be embarrassed about. Watching turns us all on." He kissed the back of her hand and she jumped as his tongue darted out, tasting her skin.

"I…I should go." She didn't move.

"No, you should watch." He dropped her hand and grabbed her shoulders, gently turning her toward the mirror. He trailed his hands up and down her arms. "Watch."

The man in the other room was now sucking on the woman's breast as his fingers caressed her pussy.

"Would you like to hear them? Or do you like it quiet?" His voice was a rough whisper against her ear.

"Sound, please." She wanted to hear their gasps and moans. She wanted to close her eyes and pretend it was her. She shifted, squeezing her thighs together.

He chuckled as he moved away. She felt his absence to her bones. He'd been strong and warm behind her and for a moment she'd felt safe, safer than she had since her brother had come back from the war, broken and sad, and her father had started drinking again.

The woman's moans filled the room and Patrick came back to stand behind her, this time placing his hands on her waist.

"I'm Patrick," he said against her ear.

She couldn't take her eyes from the scene in front of her. The woman was almost coming as the man thrust his fingers inside of her.

"What's your name?" He nipped her neck and she jumped.

"I...I..." If she told him her name, he might say something to Ethan. Ethan would kill her if he knew she was in here watching.

"Tell me your name." His lips trailed along her neck and she tipped her head giving him better access.

The guy was kissing his way down the woman's body. Annie wanted to touch herself, to make herself come but Patrick was here.

He nibbled her ear. "Why won't you tell me your name?"

"I...I'll get in trouble." She rubbed her ass against his erection, hopefully giving him a hint.

"Tease." His hand drifted down her stomach, stopping right above where she wanted him to touch. "Tell me your name or I'll make you suffer." He unbuttoned her pants and left his hand—warm, rough but immobile—resting on her abdomen.

"I can't." She stood on tip-toe, hoping his hand would lower a little but he was too tall or she was too short. He had to be almost six foot and she was barely five-foot four. "I could get fired and I need this job."

"Darling, Ethan won't fire you for fucking a customer."

"We can't." She spun around. She hadn't thought this through. He was her fantasy come to life and she wanted him to be hers just for a moment, but Ethan would find out and then she'd be in deep shit.

"Don't worry. I'm a member and you work here, so we're both clean." He hesitated, his hands tightening on her hips. "Are you protected?"

"What?" She had no idea what he was talking about.

"Ethan makes sure everyone at the Club is clean but only the…some of his employees are required to be on birth control." He ran his hands up her sides, getting closer and closer to her breasts. "Are you on birth control?" His eyes darkened as they dropped to her tits. "If not, it's okay. There are other things we can do."

Oh, she wanted to do everything his eyes promised, but she couldn't. "No, I'll get in trouble. I need this job. I have to go." She tried to move but her feet refused to obey, so she just stared at his handsome face.

"Are you sure?" He bent so he was almost eye level with her. "I promise. Ethan won't care. A lot of maids become...change jobs. The pay's a lot better." His eyes roamed over her frame. "Especially, for someone as cute as you."

Ethan would kill her before letting her become one of his pleasure associates.

"I could talk to Ethan for you." His hands moved up her body, stopping right below her breasts.

Her nipples hardened and she forgot everything but what he was making her feel. He ran his thumb over one of them and she leaned closer, wanting him to do it again.

He did. He continued rubbing her nipple as he spoke. "I could persuade him to let me...handle your initiation into club life."

Her heart raced in her chest. It could be just her and him doing all these things she'd seen. Her pussy throbbed but she couldn't do it. She wouldn't do it. She couldn't have sex for money. Her parents were both dead but they'd never understand and she couldn't disappoint them. "No. I can't do that...not for money." Her eyes darted to the door. She needed to get out of there before she did something she'd regret.

"That's even better." He smiled as he stepped closer. "We can keep this between us. No money. Only a man and a woman." He leaned down and whispered in her ear, "Giving each other pleasure. A lot of pleasure. In ways you haven't even imagined."

There were moans from the other room and she glanced over her shoulder. The man's face was buried between the woman's thighs.

Patrick turned her around, pulling her against him and wrapping his arms around her waist. "Are you wet?"

"What? No." She struggled in his arms, her ass brushing against his erection again.

"Oh fuck. Do that again." He kissed her neck, open mouthed and hot.

She stopped trying to get away. She wanted this…this moment. She shouldn't but she did, so she wiggled her butt against him again. He was hard and long and her body ached for him. It'd been too long since she'd had sex. She needed this.

"Would you like me to touch you?" His hands drifted over her hips and down her thighs.

She'd like him to do all sorts of things to her. She nodded.

"Say it." His words were a command she couldn't disobey.

"Yes."

"Yes, what?" He untucked her shirt from her pants.

"Touch me. Please." She was already pushing her hips toward his hand. She wanted his hand on her, his fingers inside of her.

"Are you wet?" he asked again.

She inhaled sharply as he unzipped her pants.

"Don't lie to me. I'll find out in a minute."

She'd never talked dirty during sex and she wasn't sure she was ready to do that with a stranger. Her heart skipped a beat. Maybe, she shouldn't be doing any of this with a stranger. She grabbed his hand. "Maybe, we shouldn't."

The woman below cried out and the man straightened, wiping his face and unbuttoning his pants.

"Watch. The main event is about to happen." Patrick's hot breath tickled her neck.

Her gaze locked on the man's penis. It was large and demanding. He straddled the woman, grabbing his cock.

"Don't you want to feel some of what they feel?" He nibbled on her ear and then neck. "I can help you."

She may not know him, but she trusted him. He was a former marine. He'd been a good friend of Vic's. He wouldn't hurt her and she needed to come. She loosened her grip, letting go of his hand. He slipped inside her pants, caressing her pussy through her underwear. His fingers were long and strong. She closed her eyes, leaning against him as he stroked her.

"You're already so wet and hot." His breath was a warm caress on her ear. "But, I'm going to make you wetter and then, I'm going to make you come." His other hand shoved her pants down, giving him more room to work. "Open your eyes and watch the show."

She did as he said. The man was inside the woman, thrusting hard and fast. The woman was moaning and trying to move but the restraints kept her mostly helpless.

"Fuck, you're soaked." Patrick's hand cupped her and she arched into his touch, rubbing her ass against his erection. He shoved his hand inside her underwear, his finger running along her folds until he slipped one inside.

"Oh." She grabbed his hand—not to push him away, but to make sure he didn't leave.

He smiled against her hair. "Don't worry, baby. I won't stop." He stroked his finger inside of her and his wrist brushed against her clit.

She needed more. She needed to touch him, feel him. She turned her head, wrapping her arms up and around his neck. He kissed her. It was desperate and wild, but he stopped too soon.

"They're almost done. You don't want to miss it."

She turned back to the mirror. The man below continued to fuck the woman as Patrick finger-fucked her. His other hand slipped under her shirt to her breast. His lips sucked her neck as he rocked his erection against her ass. He was everywhere, and she was so close. The muscles in her legs constricted. Her hips tipped upward.

"Wait, baby," he groaned in her ear, as he pushed a second finger inside of her. "Just a few more minutes."

His fingers were stretching her and it felt wonderful. She moaned, long and low as he thrust harder and faster, almost matching the pace of the man in the other room. She could almost imagine it was Patrick's cock and not his fingers inside of her.

"Oh…oh," she cried out. He was pushing her toward the edge. Her body was spiraling with each pump of his fingers. She was going to come—right here while watching that couple. It was so dirty and so wrong and it only made her hotter.

The woman below screamed and her body stiffened. The man thrust again and again and then grunted his release.

"Show's over." Patrick nipped her neck at the same time he pressed down on her clit with his thumb, sending her shooting into her orgasm.

She trembled and he pulled her close, his hand still cupping her pussy and his fingers still inside of her. When her heartbeat had settled, he removed his hand and bent, pulling off her shoes and removing her pants before lifting her and carrying her to the wall.

"My turn." He wrapped her legs around his waist.

Her phone rang. "My work phone. I…I have to answer it."

"When we're done." He unzipped his pants.

"Annie, answer the phone. I know you're around here. I can hear it ringing you stupid bitch," yelled Julie.

"Oh, shit." She shoved Patrick away, and ran across the room, grabbing her clothes off the floor. "It's my boss. She'll kill me if she finds me like this."

"I'll take care of Julie." He headed for the door, zipping up his fly. "Don't move." He grinned over his shoulder at her. "You can take off your pants again, but other than that, don't move."

"No. Please." She raced over to him, grabbing his arm. "I need this job." And Ethan could not find out about this.

"She won't fire you. She can't. Only Ethan can fire you." He bent and kissed her.

His lips were gentle and coaxing this time and her body swayed into him. He pulled her even closer and she could feel his cock, thick and heavy, pushing against her. Her pussy tightened again in anticipation.

"Damnit, Annie. This is going to be so much worse if I have to call your stupid phone again. Get out here!" Julie was only a few doors down.

She grabbed Patrick and tugged on his hand. "Please, hide." She glanced around, looking for somewhere that would conceal a six-foot muscular man.

"I'm not going to hide from Julie."

Get your free ebook and find out what happens next.
http://books2read.com/u/38r9Ka

Coming soon:

GO TO MY WEBSITE TO SEE ALL MY BOOKS AND TO SEE WHAT'S COMING NEXT
HTTPS://WWW.ELLISODAY.COM

ETHAN'S STORY
MATTIE'S STORY
A LA PETITE MORT CLUB CHRISTMAS
JAKE'S STORY
HUNTER'S STORY
DESIREE'S STORY

Email me with questions, concerns or to let me know what you thought of the book. I love hearing from readers.
authorellisoday@gmail.com

Follow me.
Facebook
https://www.facebook.com/EllisODayRomanceAuthor/

Twitter
https://twitter.com/ellis_o_day

Pinterest
www.pinterest.com\AuthorEllisODay

ABOUT THE AUTHOR

Ellis O. Day loves reading and writing about love and sex. She believes that although the two don't have to go together, it's best when they do (both in life and in fantasy).

Printed in Great Britain
by Amazon

20940723R00120